"I'm done. They can take every penny I made. I don't care." Blythe smiled. **"I have a job as of today. I don't need more than that."**

Logan liked her attitude. He just wasn't sure he believed she could go from being rich and famous to being poor and unknown.

"Anyway, it probably doesn't matter," she added with a toss of her head.

"What do you mean, it probably doesn't matter?"

Again she looked away. He reached over to turn her to face him again. "What aren't you telling me? What was the real reason you ran away with me?"

"I told you. It was my girlhood fantasy to run away with a cowboy," she said.

He shook his head. "The truth, Blythe."

She swallowed, her throat working for a moment, then she sat up a little straighter as if steeling herself. "I think someone has been trying to kill me."

USA TODAY Bestselling Author

B.J. DANIELS

CORRALLED

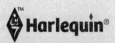

TORONTO NEW YORK LONDON
AMSTERDAM PARIS SYDNEY HAMBURG
STOCKHOLM ATHENS TOKYO MILAN MADRID
PRAGUE WARSAW BUDAPEST AUCKLAND

This is for my little brother, Charles Allen Johnson, who, like the rest of the Johnson family, has always given me something to write about.

Recycling programs
for this product may
not exist in your area.

ISBN-13: 978-0-373-69602-4

CORRALLED

Copyright © 2012 by Barbara Heinlein

www.Harlequin.com

Printed in U.S.A.

ABOUT THE AUTHOR

USA TODAY bestselling author B.J. Daniels wrote her first book after a career as an award-winning newspaper journalist and author of thirty-seven published short stories. That first book, *Odd Man Out,* received a four-and-a-half-star review from *RT Book Reviews* and went on to be nominated for Best Intrigue that year. Since then, she has won numerous awards, including a career achievement award for romantic suspense and many nominations and awards for best book.

Daniels lives in Montana with her husband, Parker, and two springer spaniels, Spot and Jem. When she isn't writing, she snowboards, camps, boats and plays tennis. Daniels is a member of Mystery Writers of America, Sisters in Crime, International Thriller Writers, Kiss of Death and Romance Writers of America.

To contact her, write to B.J. Daniels, P.O. Box 1173, Malta, MT 59538 or email her at bjdaniels@mtintouch.net. Check out her website, www.bjdaniels.com.

Books by B.J. Daniels

CAST OF CHARACTERS

Logan Chisholm—The wild Chisholm brother was hooked after one dance with a mystery woman.

Jennifer "JJ" Blythe James—Why would the famous pop singer give up everything to run away with a cowboy on a Harley?

Martin Sanderson—A lot of people wanted the hot-shot music producer dead.

Flathead County Sheriff Buford Olson—There was nothing he liked better than a good mystery or a cheeseburger loaded.

Jett Atkins—The rock star was about to be a falling star unless he could save his career, but was there something else he feared even more?

Karen "Caro" Chandler—She and JJ had been like sisters—or so she'd thought back when they started their own band.

Lisa "Luca" Thomas—The former singer/songwriter had sung her last song, but her music was destined to outlive her.

Betsy "Bets" Harper—The former keyboard player had always been the sweet one. Or at least that's what everyone thought.

Loretta "T-Top" Danvers—The former Tough as Nails drummer had her own reasons for coming to Montana.

Emma and Hoyt Chisholm—The matriarch and patriarch of Chisholm Cattle Company wanted simply to enjoy their six sons and live happily ever after. Unfortunately, someone had another plan for them.

Aggie Wells—Her greatest fear was that she would fail and Emma Chisholm would die.

Laura Chisholm—Dead or alive, she was playing havoc with the Chisholm family.

Chapter One

As he heard the music, he slowed his Harley, the throb of the engine catching the beat coming from the out-of-the-way country-western bar.

His kind of place.

He had been headed back to his hotel before that. But drawn to the music, he parked his motorcycle out front and pushed through the door into the dimly lit room. A clamor of glass and conversation competed with the band onstage.

Like him, most everyone inside was dressed in jeans and boots. The dance floor was packed, the air scented with beer and perfume as he stepped up to the bar and ordered a cold one.

Later he would recall sensing her presence even before he turned, a draft beer in hand, and first laid eyes on her.

He shoved back his Stetson, leaning against the bar, as she made her way through the crowd on the dance floor as if heading for the door. Her tight jeans hugged her hips as they swayed to the music, her full breasts pressing into the fabric of her Western shirt.

His gaze went to her boots, a pair of fancy Tony

Lama's so fresh out of the box that he could almost smell the new leather. That alone would have made him steer clear. Then he saw her face. It wasn't classically beautiful or even unusual enough to hold most men's attention.

No, but her expression of total bliss caught him like a well-thrown lasso. She stopped him in his tracks as he watched her. She was clearly lost in the music and he couldn't take his eyes off her.

When she finally looked up, her gaze locked with his. Her eyes were the color of worn jeans, her lashes dark and thick like her hair cascading from beneath her straw cowboy hat. She'd tied her hair back with a red ribbon, but loose tendrils had escaped and now framed her face.

As she started past him, impulsively he stepped in front of her. "I think you owe me a dance."

Her lips turned up in an amused smile. "Is that right?"

He nodded and, leaving his leather jacket on the bar stool, took her hand. She didn't put up a fight as he led her out onto the dance floor as one song ended. If anything, she seemed curious.

"You sure you can keep up with me?" she said challengingly as a fast song began.

He grinned, thinking the woman had no idea who she was dealing with. He was Montana born, raised on country music and cowboy jitterbug. But to his surprise, she had no trouble staying with him, giving back everything she got. He loved the way she moved with the music, all grace and sexy swing.

Everything about her surprised and thrilled him, especially the way they moved together. It was as if they were one of those older couples he'd seen in Montana bars who had danced together for years.

When the song ended and a slow dance began, she started to draw away, but he dragged her back and into his arms. She looked at him, that challenge still lighting those washed-out blue eyes of hers.

"What makes you think I don't have friends I need to get back to?" she asked as he pulled her closer, the two moving as one to the sweet sounds coming off the guitar player's strings.

"Why would you want to go back to them—if there really are people waiting for you—when you can dance with me?"

She laughed. It had a musical quality that pulled at him just as he'd been drawn to the bar band earlier.

"You are quite full of yourself," she said as if not minding it all that much.

He shook his head. "I just know there is nothing I want to do tonight but dance with you," he said honestly.

She grew serious as the song ended and another boot-stomping tune began. Her gaze locked with his as he let go of her.

"Up to you," he said quietly. Her answering smile was all invitation.

He took her hand and whirled her across the middle of the dance floor as the music throbbed, the beat matching that of his heart as he lost himself in the warm spring night, the music and this woman.

He made only one mistake as the band took a break not long before closing. He offered to buy her a drink, and when he turned back, she was gone.

As he stepped to the front door of the saloon, he was in time to see her pull away in an expensive silver convertible sports car, the top down. She glanced over at him as she left and he saw something in her expression that made him mentally kick himself for not getting her number. Or at least her name.

As she sped off, he walked back to the bar to finish his drink. He told himself that even if he had gotten her number or her name, he was only in Bigfork until tomorrow. He had to get back home to the ranch and work. But damned if he wouldn't have liked to have seen her again.

When he pulled on his leather jacket, he felt something in the pocket that hadn't been there earlier. Reaching his hand in, he pulled out a key. It wasn't like any he'd ever seen before. It was large and faux gold and had some kind of emblem on it. He couldn't make it out in the dim light of the bar, but he had a pretty good idea who'd put it in his jacket.

Finishing his beer, he pocketed the key again and left. As he climbed onto his bike, all he could think about was the woman. He couldn't remember a night when he'd had more fun or been more intrigued. Did she expect him to know what the key went to or how to find her? She expected a lot from this country boy, he thought with a smile.

He was still smiling as he cruised back to his hotel. The key was a challenge, and Logan Chisholm liked nothing better than a challenge. But if she was waiting for him tonight, she'd have a long wait.

THE NEXT MORNING LOGAN woke to see the key lying on the nightstand next to his bed. He'd tossed it there last night after taking a good look at it. He'd had no more idea what it went to than he had at the bar.

Now, though, he picked it up and ran his fingers over the raised emblem as he thought about the woman from the bar. He needed to get back to Whitehorse, back to work on his family's ranch, Chisholm Cattle Company. The last thing he needed was to go chasing after a woman he'd met on a country-western bar's dance floor miles from home.

But damned if he could leave the Flathead without finding her.

"Have you ever seen one of these?" Logan asked the hotel clerk downstairs.

"I'm sorry, Mr. Chisholm, I—"

"Isn't that a key to the Grizzly Club?" asked another clerk who'd been standing nearby. "Sorry to interrupt," he said. "But I have a friend who stayed out there once."

"The Grizzly Club?" Logan asked.

"It's an exclusive gated community south of here," the clerk said. "Very elite. You have to have five million dollars to even apply for a home site inside the development. A lot of famous people prefer that kind of privacy. There are only a few of these gated communities in Montana."

Logan knew about the one down by Big Sky. He thought about the woman at the bar last night. He couldn't see her living there, but he supposed it was possible she'd hooked up with some rich dude who'd invented computer chips or made a bundle as a famous news broadcaster. Or hell, maybe she invented the chip.

It wasn't like he really knew her after only a few dances on a spring Friday night at a country-western bar, was it?

He thought it more likely that she was a guest at the club. At least he liked that better than the other possibilities. "So you're saying this key will get me into the place?"

The clerk shook his head. "That key is to the amenities once you get inside. You don't need a key to get in the gate. There is a guard at the front gate. If someone lost their key, the guard might be able to tell you who it belongs to. I noticed it did have a number on it."

Logan didn't like the sound of a guard, but what did he have to lose? "How do I get there?"

Outside, he swung onto his bike and headed down Highway 35 south along the east side of Flathead Lake. The road was narrow, one side bordering the lake, the other rising steeply into the Mission Mountain Range. Flathead was the largest freshwater lake in the western United States, just slightly larger than Lake Tahoe. This morning it was a beautiful turquoise blue. Around the lake were hundreds of orchards making this part of Montana famous for its Flathead cherries.

The Grizzly Club sign was so small and tasteful that he almost missed the turn. The freshly paved road curled up into the mountains through dense, tall, dark pines. Logan always felt closed in by country like this because it was so different from where he lived. The Chisholm Cattle Company ranch sat in the middle of rolling Montana prairie where a man could see forever.

At home, the closest mountains were the Little Rockies, and those only a purple outline in the distance. Trees, other than cottonwoods along the Milk River and creeks, were few and far between. He loved the wide-open spaces, liked being able to see to the horizon, so he was glad when the trees finally opened up a little.

He slowed as he came to a manned gate. Beyond it, he could make out a couple of mansions set back in the trees. Was it possible one of them was owned by the woman he'd met last night? That could explain the new boots, since few people in this kind of neighborhood were from here—let alone lived here year-around.

He tried to imagine her living behind these gates even for a few weeks out of the year and decided she had to be visiting someone. A woman like that couldn't stand being locked up for long, he told himself.

The guard was on the phone and motioned for him to wait. Logan stared through the ornate iron gate and realized that the woman he was looking for could work here. And that expensive sports car convertible she was driving? She could have borrowed her boss's car last night.

He smiled. And like Cinderella, she'd had to get the car back before morning or suffer the consequences. Now that seemed more like the woman he'd met last night, he thought with a chuckle.

The guard finished his conversation and turning, perused Logan's leathers and the Harley motorcycle. He instantly looked wary. Logan realized this had been a mistake. No way was this man going to let him in or give him the name of the woman connected to the key. More than likely, the guard would call security. The best he could see coming out of this was being turned away—but only after he'd made a fool of himself.

Fortunately, he didn't get the chance. From the other side of the gate, he saw the flash of a small silver sports car convertible coming through the trees. The top was still down. He caught a glimpse of the driver.

She'd done away with her cowboy attire, including the hat. Her hair blew free, forming a wave like a raven's wing behind her as she sped toward the gate. She wore large sunglasses that hid most of her face, but there was no denying it was the woman from the bar.

"Never mind," Logan said to the guard and swung his bike around as the gate automatically opened on the other side of the guardhouse and the sports car roared out.

Logan went after her.

He couldn't believe how fast she was driving, taking the curves with abandon. He saw her glance in her rearview mirror and speed up. Logan did the same, the two of them racing down out of the mountains and onto the narrow road along the lake.

This woman is crazy, Logan thought when she hit the narrow two-lane highway and didn't slow down. She wanted to race? Then they would race.

He stayed right with her, roaring up beside her when there was no traffic. She would glance at him, then gun it, forcing him to fall behind her when an oncoming car appeared.

They were almost to the town of Bigfork when she suddenly hit the brakes and whipped off the road onto a wide spot overlooking the lake. She'd barely gotten the car stopped at the edge of the rocky cliff, the water lapping at the shore twenty feet below.

Logan skidded to a stop next to her car as she jumped out and, without a word, climbed onto the back of his bike. Wrapping her arms around his waist, she leaned into him and whispered, "Get me out of here."

After that exhilarating race, she didn't need to ask twice. He was all the more intrigued by this woman. He roared back onto the highway headed north toward Glacier National Park. As she pressed her body against his, he heard her let out a sigh, and wondered where they were headed both literally and figuratively.

Caught up in the moment, he breathed in the cool mountain air. It smelled of spring and new beginnings. He loved this time of year. Just as he loved the feel of the woman on the bike behind him.

The sun was warm as it scaled the back of the Mission Mountains and splashed down over Flathead Lake. At the north end of the lake, Logan pulled into a small out-of-the-way café that he knew catered to fishermen. "Hungry?"

She hesitated only a moment, then nodded, smiling, as she followed him into the café. He ordered them both the breakfast special, trout, hash browns, eggs and toast with coffee and watched her doctor her coffee with both sugar and cream.

"Are you at least going to tell me your name?" he asked as they waited for their order.

She studied him. "That depends. Do you live around here?"

He shook his head. "East of here, outside of a town called Whitehorse." He could tell she'd never heard of it. "It's in the middle of nowhere, a part of Montana most tourists never see."

"You think I'm a tourist?" She smiled at that.

"Aren't you?" He still couldn't decide if she was visiting the Grizzly Club or lived there with her rich husband. But given the way she'd left that expensive sports car beside the lake, he thought his present-day Cinderella theory might not be that far off base.

Maybe he just didn't want to believe it, but he was convinced she wasn't married to some tycoon. She hadn't been wearing a wedding ring last night or today. Not only that, she didn't act married—or in a committed relationship. Not that he hadn't been wrong about that before.

"Don't you think you should at least tell me your name?" he asked.

She looked around the café for a moment as if considering telling him her name. When those pale blue eyes came back to him, she said, "Blythe. That's my name."

"Nice to meet you, Blythe." He reached across the table extending his hand. "Logan. You have a last name?"

Her hand felt small and warm in his. She didn't clean houses at the Grizzly Club, that was definite, he thought, as he felt her silky-smooth palm. Several silver bracelets jingled lightly on her slim tanned wrist. But she could still be a car thief.

"Blythe is good enough for now, don't you think?"

"I guess it depends on what happens next."

She grinned. "What would you like to happen next?"

"I'm afraid I have to head back home today, otherwise I might have had numerous suggestions."

"Back to Whitehorse," she said studying him. "Someone waiting for you back there?"

"Nope." He could have told her about his five brothers and his father and stepmother back at the ranch, but he knew that wasn't what she'd meant. He'd also learned the hard way not to mention Chisholm Cattle Company. He'd seen too many dollar signs appear in some women's eyes. There was a price to be paid when you were the son of one of the largest ranch owners in the state.

"Someone waiting for *you* back at the Grizzly Club?" he asked.

"Nope."

Their food arrived then and she dived into hers as if she hadn't eaten in a week. She might not have, he realized. He had no idea who this woman was or what was going to happen next, but he didn't care. He liked her, liked watching her eat. She did it with the same kind of passion and abandon she'd shown dancing and driving.

"I've never seen that part of Montana," she said as they were finishing. She wiped her expressive mouth and tossed down her napkin. "Show me."

He raised a brow. "It's a five-hour drive from here."

When she didn't respond, he asked, "What about your car?"

"It's a rental. I'll call and have the agency collect it."

He considered her for a moment. "You don't want to pick up anything from your house?"

"It's not my house, and I like to travel light."

Logan still wasn't sure she was serious about going with him, but serious or not, he was willing to take her up on whatever she was offering. He liked that he had no idea who she was, what she wanted or what she would do next. It had been too long since a woman had captivated him to the point that he was willing to throw caution to the wind.

"Let's ride then." As they left the café, he couldn't help but notice the way she looked around as if afraid of who might be waiting for her outside. He was reminded of how she'd come flying out of the Grizzly Club. Maybe she really had stolen that car she'd been driving and now he was harboring a criminal.

He laughed to himself. He was considered the rebel Chisholm brother. The one who'd always been up for any adventure, whether it was on horseback or a Harley. But as they walked to his motorcycle, he had a bad feeling that he might be getting into more than even he could handle.

Chapter Two

Sheriff Buford Olson hitched up his pants over his expanding belly, reached back into his patrol car for his Stetson and, closing the door, tilted his head back to look up at the hotel-size building called the Main Lodge.

Buford hated getting calls to come out to the Grizzly Club. It wasn't that he disliked the rich, although he did find them demanding and damned irritating.

It was their private security force, a bunch of punk kids, who made his teeth ache. Buford considered anyone under thirty-five to be a kid. The "club" had given these kids a uniform and a gun and turned them into smart-ass, dangerous punks who knew diddly-squat about law enforcement.

Buford always wondered why the club had to call him in if their security force was so capable. It was no secret that the club liked to handle its own problems. The people who owned homes inside the gates didn't want anyone outside them knowing their business. So the whole idea was to sweep whatever trouble the club had under one of their expensive Persian rugs.

Worse, the folks who owned the club didn't want to

upset the residents—or jeopardize new clientele—so they wanted everyone to believe that once they were behind these gates they were safe and nothing bad could happen.

Buford snorted at the thought, recalling how the general manager had asked him to park in the back of the main lodge so he wouldn't upset anyone. The guard at the gate had said, "Sheriff Buford, right? I heard you were here for a complimentary visit."

A complimentary visit. That had made him contrary enough that he'd parked right out front of "the Main Lodge." Now, though, as he started up the wide flagstone steps, he wished he hadn't been so obstinate. He felt his arthritis bothering him and, worse, his stomach roiling against the breakfast his wife had cooked him.

Clara had read in one of her magazines that if you ate a lot of hot peppers it would make you lose weight. She'd been putting hot chile peppers in everything they ate—and playing hell with his stomach.

The general manager he'd spoken to earlier spotted him and came rushing toward him. The diminutive man, whose name Buford couldn't recall at first, was painfully thin with skin that hadn't seen sunlight and piercing blue eyes that never settled more than a second.

"I thought I told you to park in the back."

Buford shrugged. "So what's the problem?" he asked as he looked around the huge reception area. All the leather, antler lamps and chandeliers, thick rugs and gleaming wood floors reminded him of Clara's designer magazines.

Montana style, they called it. The Lodge Look. Buford was old enough to remember when a lot of places looked like this, only they'd been the real McCoy—not this forced Montana style.

"In here," the general manager ordered, drawing him into a small, claustrophobic office with only one window that looked out on the dense forest. The name on the desk read Kevin Andrews, General Manager.

Kevin closed the door and for the first time, Buford noticed how nervous the man appeared. The last time Buford had been called here was for a robbery inside the gates. That time he'd thought Kevin was going to have a heart attack, he'd been so upset. But once the missing jewelry, which turned out only to have been misplaced, was found, all was well and quickly forgotten.

Buford guessed though that it had taken ten years off Kevin's life from the looks of him. "So what's up? More missing jewelry?"

"This is a very delicate matter. I need you to handle it with the utmost care. Do I have your word?"

Buford felt his stomach roil again. He was in no mood for this. "Just tell me what's happened."

The general manager rose from his chair with a brisk "come with me."

Buford followed him out to a golf cart. Resigned that he had no choice but to ride along, he climbed on. Kevin drove them through the ritzy residence via the narrow paved roads that had been hacked out of the pines.

The hotel-size houses were all set back from the

road, each occupying at least ten acres from Buford's estimation since the buildings had to take up three of those acres with guest houses of another half acre. Each log, stone and glass structure was surrounded by pine trees so he only caught glimpses of the exclusive houses as Kevin whipped along the main road.

Finally he pulled down one of the long driveways, coming to a stop in front of a stone monstrosity with two wide wooden doors. Like the others, the house was all rock and logs with massive windows that looked out over the pines on the mountainside and Flathead Lake far below.

Buford saw with a curse that two of the security force's golf carts were parked out front. One of the garage doors was open. A big, black SUV hunkered in one of the three stalls. The others were empty.

Getting off the golf cart, he let Kevin lead him up to the front door. Bears had been carved into the huge wooden doors, and not by some roadside chainsaw artist. Without knocking, Kevin opened the door and Buford followed him inside.

He was hit at once with a familiar smell and felt his stomach clutch. This was no missing jewelry case.

With dread, he moved across the marble floor to where the walls opened into a football field–size living room with much the same furnishings as the club's main lodge. The two security guards were standing at the edge of the room. They had been visiting, but when they saw Kevin, they tried to act professional.

Buford looked past them to the dead man sprawled beside the hearth of the towering rock fireplace. The deceased was wearing a white, blood-soaked velour robe and a pair of leather slippers on his feet. Apparently nothing else.

"Get them out of here," Buford ordered, pointing at the two security guards. He could only guess at how many people had already tromped through here contaminating the scene. "Stay back and make sure no one else comes traipsing through here."

He swore under his breath as he worked his way across the room to the fireplace and the dead man. The victim looked to be in his late fifties, but could have been older because, from the tightness of his facial skin, he'd had some work done. His hair was dark with distinguishing gray at the temples, a handsome man even in death.

It appeared he'd been shot in the heart at point-blank range. An expensive handgun lay on the floor next to the body in a pool of drying blood. Clearly the man had been dead for hours. Buford swore again. He'd bet that Kevin had contacted the Grizzly Club board before he'd called the sheriff's department.

Around the dead man were two different distinct prints left in his blood. One was a man-size dress shoe sole. The other a cowboy boot—small enough that Buford would guess it was a woman's. It was her prints that held his attention. The woman hadn't walked away—she'd run—straight for the front door.

AT THE MOTORCYCLE, BLYTHE tied up her hair and climbed on behind the cowboy. She didn't think about what she was doing as she wrapped her arms around him. All she knew was that she had to escape, and wherever Logan was headed was fine with her. Even better, this Whitehorse place sounded like the end of the earth. With luck, no one would find her there.

She reminded herself that she'd thought this part of Montana would be far from the life she wanted so desperately to leave behind. But she'd been wrong.

Running didn't come easy to her. She'd always been a fighter. But not today. Today she only wanted to forget everything, hang on to this good-looking cowboy on the back of his motorcycle, feel the wind in her face and put her old life as far behind her as possible.

An image flashed in her mind, making her shudder, and she glanced down at her cowboy boots. She quickly wiped away a streak of dark red along the sole as Logan turned the key and brought the Harley to life.

She felt the throb of the engine and closed her eyes and her mind the way she used to tune out her mother when she was a girl. Back then it was to close out the sound of her mother and her latest boyfriend arguing in the adjacent room of the small, old trailer house. She had learned to go somewhere else, be *someone* else, always dreaming of a fantasy life far away.

With a smile, she remembered that one of her daydreams had been to run away with a cowboy. The thought made her hold on to Logan tighter as he shifted and tore out of the café parking lot in a shower of gravel.

Last night dancing with Logan she'd thought she was finally free. It was the best she'd felt in years. Now she pressed her cheek into the soft warmth of his leather jacket, lulled by the pulse of the motorcycle, the feel of the wind in her hair. She couldn't believe that he'd found her.

What had she been thinking giving him that damned key? She'd taken a terrible risk, but then she'd never dreamed he would come looking for her. What if he had gotten into the Grizzly Club this morning before she'd gotten out of there?

She shook off the thought and watched the countryside blur past, first forest-covered mountains, then wide-open spaces as they raced along the two-lane highway that cut east across the state.

She'd gotten away. No one knew where she was. But still she had to look back. The past had been chasing her for so long, she didn't kid herself that it wasn't close behind.

There were no cars close behind them, but that didn't mean that they wouldn't be looking for her.

For a moment, she considered what she'd done. She didn't know this cowboy, didn't know where he was taking her or what would happen when they got there.

This is so like you. Leaping before you look. Not thinking about the consequences of your actions. As if you weren't in enough trouble already.

Her mother's words rang in her ears. The only difference this time was that she wasn't that fourteen-year-old girl with eleven dollars in the pocket of her worn jean jacket and her only possession a beat-up guitar one of her mother's boyfriend's had left behind.

She'd escaped both times. That time from one of her

mother's amorous boyfriends and with her virginity. This time with her life. At least so far.

That reckless spirit is going to get you into trouble one day. You mark my words, girl.

Wouldn't her mama love to hear that she'd been right. But mama was long dead and Jennifer Blythe James was still alive. If anything, that girl and the woman she'd become was a survivor. She'd gotten out of that dirty desert trailer park where she'd started life. She would get out of this.

"WHO'S THE VICTIM?" Sheriff Buford Olson asked, sensing the Grizzly Club general manager hovering somewhere at a discreet distance behind him.

"Martin Sanderson," Kevin said. "It's his house."

Buford studied the larger bloody footprint next to the body. At a glance, he could see that it didn't match the soles of the two security guards or the general manager's, and unlike the other smaller print, this one headed not for the door, but in the opposite direction.

As he let his gaze follow the path the bloody prints had taken, Buford noted that the man had tried to wipe his shoe clean of the blood on an expensive-looking rug between the deceased and the bar where he was now lounging.

Buford was startled to see the man making himself at home at the bar with a drink in his hand. How many people had those dumb security guards let in?

"What the hell?" the sheriff demanded as he pushed himself up from where he'd been squatting beside the body. The "club" gave him a royal pain. He moved toward the bar, being careful not to step on the bloody footprints the man had left behind.

Buford didn't need to ask the man's name. He recognized Jett Akins only because his fourteen-year-old granddaughter Amy had a poster of the man on her bedroom wall. On the poster, Jett had been wearing all black—just as he was this morning—and clutching a fancy electric guitar. Now he clutched a tumbler, the dark contents only half full.

The one time his granddaughter had played a Jett Atkin's song for him, Buford had done his best not to show his true feelings. The so-called song had made him dearly miss the 1960s. Seemed to him there hadn't been any good music since then, other than country-western, of course.

"Mr. Atkins found the body," Kevin said from the entryway.

Jett Atkins looked pale and shaken. He downed the rest of his drink as the sheriff came toward him. Buford would guess it wasn't his first.

"You found the body?" he asked Jett, who looked older than he had on his poster. He had dark hair and eyes and a large spider tattoo on his neck and more tattoos on the back of his hands—all that was showing since the black shirt he wore was long-sleeved.

"I flew in this morning and took a taxi here. When I saw Martin, I called the club's emergency number." His voice died off as he looked again at the dead man by the fireplace and poured himself another drink.

Buford wanted to ask why the hell he hadn't called 911 instead of calling the club's emergency number. Isn't that what a normal person would do when he found a dead body?

He turned to Kevin again. "How many people were in this house?"

"Mr. Sanderson had left the names of six approved guests at the gate with the guard, along with special keys for admittance to all the amenities on the grounds," Kevin said in his annoyingly official tone. "All of those keys have been picked up."

"*Six* people? So where are they?" the sheriff demanded. "And I am going to need a list of their names." Before he could finish, Kevin withdrew a folded sheet of paper from his pocket and stepped around the sunken living room to hand it to him.

"These are the names of the guests Mr. Sanderson approved."

Buford read off the names. "JJ, Caro, Luca, Bets, T-Top and Jett. Those aren't *names.*" He had almost forgotten about Jett until he spoke.

"They're stage names," he said. "Caro, Luca, T-Top, and Bets. It's from when they were in a band together."

Stage names? "Are they actors?" Buford asked, thinking things couldn't get any worse.

"Musicians," Jett said.

He was wrong about things not getting worse. He couldn't tell the difference between women's or men's names and said as much.

"They were an all-girl band back in the nineties called Tough as Nails," Jett said, making it sound as if the nineties were the Stone Age.

"You don't know their *real* names?" Buford asked.

"They are the only names required for our guards to admit them," Kevin said. "Here at the Grizzly Club we respect the privacy of our residents."

Swearing, Buford wrote down: Caro, Luca, T-Top and Bets in his notebook.

"What about this JJ?" he asked. "You said he picked up his key yesterday?"

"She."

Buford turned to look at Jett. "She?" he asked thinking one of these women account for the woman's cowboy-boot print in the dead man's blood.

"JJ. She was also in the band, the lead singer," Jett said.

The sheriff turned to the club manager again. "I need full legal names for these guests and I need to know where they are."

"Only Mr. Sanderson would have that information and he… All I can tell you is that the five approved guests picked up their amenities keys yesterday. This gentleman picked his up at the gate today at 1:16 p.m.," he said, indicating Jett.

"Which means the others are all here inside the gates?" Buford asked.

Kevin checked the second sheet of paper he'd taken from a separate pocket. "All except JJ. She left this morning at 10:16 a.m."

Buford glanced over at the body. 10:16 a.m. That had to be close to the time of the murder, since the dead man's blood was still wet when a woman wearing cowboy boots appeared to have knelt by the body, then sprinted for the front door.

* * *

Blythe pressed her cheek against Logan's broad back and breathed in the rich scents on the cool spring air. The highway rolled past in a blur, the hours slipping by until they were cruising along the Rocky Mountain front, the high mountain peaks snow-capped and beautiful.

The farther Blythe and Logan traveled, the fewer vehicles they saw. When they stopped at a café in the small western town of Cut Bank along what Logan said was called the Hi-Line, she was ravenous again.

"Not many people live up here, huh," she said as she climbed off the bike. A fan pumped the smell of grease out the side of the café. She smiled to herself as she realized how much she'd missed fried food. All those years of dieting seemed such a waste right now.

"You think *this* is isolated?" Logan said with a chuckle. "Wait until you see where we're headed. They say there are only .03 people per square mile. I suspect it's less."

She smiled, shaking her head as she tried to imagine such wide-open spaces. Even when she'd lived in the desert there had been a large town closeby. Since then she'd lived in congested cities. The thought of so few people seemed like heaven.

Blythe could tell Logan wanted to ask where she was from, but she didn't give him a chance as she turned and headed for the café door. She'd seen a few pickups parked out front, but when she pushed open the door, she was surprised to find the café packed.

One of the waitresses spotted her, started to come

over, then did a double take. She burst into a smile. "I know you. You're—"

"Mistaken," Blythe said, cutting the girl off, sensing Logan right behind her.

The girl looked confused and embarrassed. "I don't have a table ready. But you look so much like—"

Blythe hated being rude, but she turned around and took Logan's arm. "I'm too hungry to wait," she said as she pulled him back through the door outside again.

"Did you know that waitress?" Logan asked, clearly taken aback by the way she'd handled it. "She seemed to know you."

She shook her head. "I must have one of those faces or that waitress has been on her feet too long. I didn't mean to be abrupt with her. I get cranky when I'm hungry. Can we go back to that barbecue place we passed?" She turned and headed for the bike before he could press the subject.

"You sure you've never been to this town before?" he asked as he swung onto the bike.

"Positive," she said as she climbed on behind him. It wasn't until he started the bike that she let herself glance toward the front windows of the café. The young waitress was standing on the other side of the glass.

Blythe looked away, promising herself that she would make it up to her one day. *If she was still alive.*

She shoved that thought away, realizing she should have known someone would recognize her even though she looked different now. It was the eyes, she thought, and closed them as Logan drove back to the barbecue joint.

It wasn't until later, after they'd settled into a booth and ordered, that she tried to smooth things over with Logan. She could tell he was even more curious about her. And suspicious, as well.

"When I was a little girl I used to watch old Westerns on television," she said, hoping to lighten both of their moods. "I always wanted to run away with a cowboy."

"So you're a romantic."

She laughed softly as she looked across the table at him. There were worry lines between the brows of his handsome face.

"Or was it the running away part that appealed to you?" he asked.

"That could definitely be part of it. Haven't you ever wanted to run away?"

"Sure." His Montana blue-sky eyes bore into her. "Most people don't have the luxury of actually doing it though."

"Good thing we aren't most people," she said, giving him a flirtatious smile.

"Oh? You think we're that much alike? So tell me what *you're* like and I'll tell you whether or not you're right about me."

"No big mystery. I like to dance, drive fast, have a good time and I'm always up for an adventure. How else could I have ended up living that little-girl fantasy of running away with a cowboy?"

"How else indeed," Logan said, but he was smiling.

"HAS ANYONE LOOKED IN this house for the four approved guests who are unaccounted for?" the sheriff demanded.

Kevin was reaching for his phone to check with his security personnel when Buford caught a glint out of the corner of his eye. Turning toward Sanderson's body, he saw something glittering on the lapel of the dead man's robe that he hadn't noticed before.

Stepping over to the body again, he crouched down next to Sanderson and inspected the lapel. Someone had attached a safety pin to the left-hand lapel of the dead man's robe. As Buford looked closer, he found a tiny piece of yellow paper still attached to it.

The killer had left a note? Or was it possible that Sanderson had left a suicide note?

The thought took him by surprise. He'd been treating this like a homicide. But what if it had been a suicide, complete with note?

If so, then why would anyone take it? To protect Sanderson? To purposely make it appear to be a homicide?

A history buff, Buford thought of a famous death that perplexed historians still. Captain Meriwether Lewis of the famed Lewis and Clark Expedition through Montana had suffered from depression that was thought to be the cause of his apparent suicide. But there were still those who believed he'd been murdered.

Very perplexing, Buford thought as he moved to a small desk in the kitchen. On it was a yellow sticky note pad. The top sheet had been torn in half horizontally, leaving the glued piece and a ragged edge. The paper was the same color as the tiny scrap still caught on the safety pin.

A blue pen lay beside the pad. Unfortunately there

was no slight indentation on the pad. Whoever had written the note had ripped the scrap of paper off first before writing the note.

"Did anyone remove something that had been pinned to the deceased's robe?" he asked. Both Kevin, the two guards and Jett swore they hadn't. From their surprise at the question, Buford suspected they were telling the truth.

But *someone* had taken the note.

Chapter Three

"So tell me about your life in this isolated place where you live," Blythe said, steering the conversation away from her as they waited for their barbecue sandwiches.

Clearly Logan was itching to know who he'd let climb onto the back of his bike. Not that she could blame him. But she wasn't ready to tell him—if she ever did. Better to split before that.

"Not much to tell," he said, as if being as evasive as she was. "I spend most days with cows. Seems I'm either chasing them, feeding them, branding them, birthing them, inoculating them or mending the fence to keep them in."

"Sounds wonderful."

He laughed. "You obviously haven't worked on a ranch."

The waitress brought their orders and Blythe dived into hers. As she stole a look across the table at him, she thought about how he'd come looking for her at the Grizzly Club, how he hadn't batted an eyelash when she'd suggested going with him, how he hadn't really asked anything of her—not even what the devil she was doing taking off across Montana with a stranger. He probably thought she did this kind of thing all the time.

A thought chilled her to her bones. What if it was no coincidence that he'd come into her life last night?

No, she thought as she studied him. The cowboy had no idea who she was or what he was getting himself into.

She jumped as her cell phone blurted out a song she'd come to hate. Worse, she hadn't even realized she still had the phone in her jacket pocket. She'd thought she'd left it along with her purse and the keys in the car.

Logan was looking at her expectantly. "Aren't you going to take that?"

She had no choice. She reached into her pocket. As she pulled out the phone, the scrap of wadded up yellow note paper fell out. It tumbled under the booth.

The first few refrains of the song began again. She hurriedly turned the phone off without even bothering to check who was calling. She had a pretty good idea, not that it mattered.

The song died off, the silence in the café almost painful, but she saw a girl at the counter looking at her frowning slightly as if trying to either place the song— or her. The girl, Blythe had noticed earlier, had been visiting with the cook.

"What if that was important?" Logan asked.

"It wasn't."

She picked up her fork and began eating again, even though she'd lost her appetite. She could feel his gaze on her. She thought about the scrap of notepaper she'd dropped and what had been written on it. She had shoved it into her pocket earlier and forgotten about it.

"Won't someone miss you?"

"I really doubt it." She moved her food around her plate, pretending to still be interested in eating, and fortunately he let the subject drop. As soon as she could, she excused herself to go to the bathroom. When she returned, Logan was up at the counter paying for their meal.

The girl at the counter was staring at her again as if it wouldn't take much to place where she knew her from. She had to get that stupid song off her phone.

Blythe glanced toward the booth. She couldn't see the scrap of notepaper. Nor could she get down on her hands and knees to look for it without raising all kinds of questions.

Not to worry, she assured herself. The note would get swept out with the garbage tonight. What had she been thinking hanging on to it anyway?

That was just it. She hadn't been thinking. She'd just been running for her life.

BUFORD CAUGHT JETT MAKING a call on his cell. "Hey, I don't know who you're trying to call, but don't. You'll get a chance to call your lawyer, if I decide to arrest you."

"Arrest me?" Jett said pocketing his phone. "*I* didn't kill him."

Buford heard a noise from down a long hallway toward the back of the house. He turned to see three women headed toward the sunken living room—and the murder scene.

He moved quickly to cut them off as the tall blonde in front glanced at his uniform and asked, "What's going on?"

"I'm Sheriff Buford Olson," he said introducing himself and shielding the woman from Martin Sanderson's body. "Where did the three of you come from?"

"The guesthouse out back," the blonde said frowning. "Where's Martin?"

"I need to speak to each of you." Buford turned to the club's general manager, amazed Kevin and his security force hadn't thought to search the house, let alone the guesthouse out back. "Kevin, can you suggest a place I can speak with these women?"

"Mr. Sanderson's library. Or perhaps his office?"

The sheriff motioned for Kevin to lead the way. They backtracked down the hallway toward the back of the huge house, the same way the women had come. Buford left the general manager in the plush library with instructions to say nothing to the other two women, while he took the blonde across the hall to Sanderson's office.

"What is this about?" she wanted to know.

"If you would have a seat," he said. "I need to ask you a few questions, beginning with your name."

She sat down reluctantly and looked around as if searching for something. At his puzzled frown, she said, "I was hoping there would be an ashtray in here." She pulled out a pack of cigarettes, seemed to think better of it and put them back into her jacket pocket.

Buford studied her as she did so. She said her name

was Loretta Danvers, aka T-Top because of a hairdo she'd had ten years ago when she played in the band Tough as Nails. She was thirty-something, tall, thin and bleached blond. In her face was etched the story of a hard life.

"So what's this about?" she asked again.

"Martin Sanderson is dead," he said and watched her reaction.

She laughed. "Isn't that the way my luck goes? So the reunion tour is off? Or was it ever really on?"

"The reunion tour?"

"He was putting our old band together for a reunion tour. At least that's what he said." She pulled out her cigarettes, shook one out and lit it with a cheap lighter. "Guess he won't care if I smoke then, will he." She took a drag, held it in her lungs for a long moment and then released a cloud of smoke out of the corner of her mouth away from him. "With JJ onboard, we could have finally made some money. I knew it was too good to be true. So who killed him?"

"Do you know someone who wanted him dead?"

She laughed again. "Who *didn't* want him dead?"

You, apparently, Buford thought, since with Sanderson gone, so apparently was any chance of a reunion tour.

LOGAN DIDN'T START HAVING real misgivings until after Blythe's phone call. He hadn't even realized that she'd brought her cell phone until it had gone off. It wasn't until then that he'd recalled that she'd said she would have someone pick up the car she'd left beside Flathead

Lake, but he hadn't seen her call anyone. In fact, he'd gotten the impression when the phone began to play that song that she hadn't even remembered that she had the phone with her.

Who had been calling? Someone she hadn't been interested in talking to. Even the ring tone with that pop-rock-sounding song didn't seem like her. Was it even her phone?

He'd realized then too that Blythe hadn't only left an expensive sports car convertible behind. She'd apparently left her purse, as well. What woman left behind her purse in a convertible beside the road? Or had she left it at the Grizzly Club?

After recalling the way she'd come flying out of club, he couldn't shake the feeling that maybe she wasn't as freewheeling as he'd originally thought—and instead was running from something serious. What did he really know about this woman he was taking back to Whitehorse with him?

Every time he'd started to ask her anything personal, she'd avoided answering one way or another. When he'd seen her reach for her cell phone, he'd noticed that she'd dropped something under the booth. He saw her look for it, then, as if changing her mind, go to the restroom. He had waited until the door closed behind her before he'd retrieved what she'd dropped.

It was nothing more than a crumpled scrap of paper from a yellow sticky notepad. He felt foolish for picking it up from under the booth and, as the waitress came by to clear the table, he'd hastily pocketed it without even looking to see if anything was written on it.

He'd been at the counter paying for the meal when Blythe had come out of the restroom. He saw her glance toward the booth. No, glance down as if looking under the booth to see what she'd dropped? Or hoping to retrieve it?

The woman intrigued him. Not a bad thing, he told himself as they left the café and climbed back on his motorcycle. He'd take her to Whitehorse and, if he had to, he'd buy her a bus ticket to wherever she needed to go. All his instincts told him that she needed to get away from something and he was happy to oblige. Chisholm men were suckers for women in trouble.

As she wrapped her arms around him and leaned into his back, he started the motor and took off. He tried to relax as the country opened. He felt as if he could breathe again. Whatever was up with this woman, he would deal with it when the time came.

A few hours later when he crossed into Whitehorse County, he'd forgotten about the scrap of paper in his pocket. He was too busy breathing a sigh of relief. He liked leaving, but there was nothing like coming home.

He breezed into the small Western town, thinking it would be a mistake to take her out to the house until they'd talked. At the very least, shouldn't he know her last name? He had always preferred not to take a woman to his house. Actually, he'd never met one he liked well enough to take home.

It didn't take but a few minutes to cruise down the main drag of Whitehorse. The town had been built up along the railroad line more than a hundred years ago. He waved at a few people he knew, the late afternoon sun throwing dark shadows across the buildings. He pulled into a space in front of the Whitehorse Bar and cut the engine.

"Could we just go to your house?" she asked without getting off the bike.

He looked at her over his shoulder. She had the palest blue eyes he'd ever seen. There was something vast about them. But it was the pain he saw just below the cool blue surface that took hold of him and wouldn't let go.

"You sure about this?" he asked.

She held his gaze and nodded. "Haven't you ever just needed to step out of your life for a while and take a chance?"

He smiled at that. Born a cowboy, riding a horse before he could walk, and now astride a Harley with a woman he probably shouldn't have been with. "Yeah, I get that."

She smiled back. "I had a feeling you might."

All his plans to get the truth out of her evaporated like a warm summer rain on hot pavement. He started the bike, flipped a U-turn in the middle of the street and headed out of town, hoping he wasn't making his worst mistake yet.

BUFORD ASKED FORMER DRUMMER Loretta Danvers to return to the guesthouse for the time being until he could talk to the others. Then he called in the next woman.

"Which one are you?" he asked the plump redhead.

Bets turned out to be Betsy Harper. He quickly

found out that she'd played the keyboard in the former all-girl band and hadn't been that sorry when the band broke up. Now, the married mother of three said she played the organ at church and kept busy with her sons' many activities.

She looked relieved more than surprised when he told her that Martin Sanderson was dead.

"Then there isn't going to be a reunion tour," she said nodding. "I can't say I'm sorry about that. I was dreading being away from my family."

Both women had mentioned the tour. "You don't seem upset by Mr. Sanderson's death," Buford said, surprised since of the three, Betsy Harper had a more caring look about her.

"I feel terrible about that," she said. "But Martin wasn't a nice man."

She didn't ask how he'd died, nor did she offer any suggestions on who would want him dead. Her only question was when she would be able to return to her husband and kids.

Buford sent her back to the guesthouse and brought in Karen "Caro" Chandler, former guitarist and singer.

She was a slim brunette with large soft brown eyes. She was the only one who looked upset when he told her that Martin Sanderson was dead.

"How did he die?" she asked, sounding worried.

"He was shot."

She shuddered. "Do you know who…?"

"Not yet. It's possible he killed himself."

She looked so relieved he questioned her about it. "I

was just worried that JJ might have…done something to him."

The elusive JJ. "Why would you say that?" he asked.

"Everyone in the business knew she was trying to get out of her contract."

The business being the music business, he guessed.

"Then there were those accidents onstage during her most recent road tour," Karen said. "Martin made it all sound like it was a publicity stunt, but I saw JJ interviewed on television. She looked genuinely scared. I was worried about her."

"You kept in touch with her over the ten years since the band broke up?"

"No," she said quickly with a shake of her head. "I'm sure the others told you that we didn't part on the best of terms. The band broke up shortly after JJ left. She was obviously the talent behind it."

Both Loretta and Betsy had made it clear they hadn't been in contact with JJ since the breakup, either.

"Not that I blamed JJ," she said quickly. "Who wouldn't have jumped at an opportunity like that if Martin Sanderson had offered it to them?"

BUFORD SENT KAREN TO THE guesthouse after the interview. All three had claimed the same thing. They'd all arrived by taxi together and had been together the entire time—except for when they'd gone into separate rooms in the guesthouse to sleep.

They said Martin had told them to relax and take advantage of the club's facilities. He would meet with them the next afternoon at two. He had said he had other business to take care of this morning and didn't wish to be disturbed.

All said they had come to Montana because Martin Sanderson was paying their expenses and promising them a reunion tour of their former band.

"What about this morning?" the sheriff had asked each of them. They had gone to bed early, had breakfast in the guest quarters and hadn't heard a sound coming from the main house.

The blonde, Loretta, said she'd been the first one down to breakfast but that she'd heard the showers running in both rooms as she'd passed. The other two, Betsy and Karen, had come down shortly thereafter.

The three hadn't been apart except to go to the bathroom since then.

Buford figured any one of them could have sneaked out to go to the main house and wasn't ruling any of them out if Martin Sanderson's death was found to be a homicide.

"Where is the other member of your former band?" Buford asked and checked his list. "Luca."

"Dead," the blonde said. "Talk about bad luck. Stepped out in front of a bus."

"How does Jett fit in?" he'd asked Betsy.

"Didn't he tell you? He used to hang around the band, flirting with all of us, but in the end, he left with JJ when she left the band. As far as I know, they're still together. At least according to the tabloids I see at the grocery checkout. I don't read them, mind you."

All of them swore they hadn't seen JJ and claimed they weren't even aware that she had arrived yet. When

he'd checked the other rooms of the house, he found a
guest room at the far end of the house where someone
had obviously spent the night. The room was far enough
away from the living room that Buford suspected a gunshot couldn't be heard.

He waited until the coroner and crime scene techs
took over before he interviewed Jett Atkins. By then,
Jett had had enough to drink that he was feeling no
pain.

"So did one of them confess?" he asked with a laugh.
"I didn't think so. They know who killed Martin. JJ."

"Why do you say that?"

Jett looked shocked. "It's been in all the trades for
months. JJ wanted out of her contract. Martin refused.
We all knew it was coming to a head. Why else would
he threaten to put her old band back together?"

"*Threaten?* I thought he flew everyone up here to
make arrangements for the tour," the sheriff said.

Jett howled with laughter. "There is no way JJ would
ever have agreed to that. No, he was just trying to bring
her back in line. Those women hate JJ. She not only
broke up the band, she also became successful. I would
imagine JJ went ballistic when Martin told her that
either she played ball or he would force her into doing
a reunion tour with women who would have stabbed
her in the back just as quickly as looked at her."

"Martin Sanderson could make her do that?"

"He *owned* her. He could do anything he wanted.
The only way she could get out of that contract was to
die. Or," Jett added with a grin. "Kill Martin."

"Do you think this JJ knew that Martin had already

flown the band members to Montana?" Buford asked. All except Luca, whoever she had been.

"Doubt it, since apparently he had them staying in a separate guest house," Jett said. "I can't say I blame JJ for killing him. He really was a bastard."

"What about you?" Buford asked.

"What about me?"

"What are you doing here?"

"Martin invited me." He grinned. "More leverage. I'm sure he planned to leak it to the press. He wanted it to look like JJ and I were back together."

"You weren't?"

He shook his head. "It was just a publicity stunt. Martin loved doing them. But JJ and I would have had to go along with it, since he held our contracts."

"So you were signed with him, as well. How does his death affect that?"

Jett smiled widely. "Freedom. With Martin dead, JJ and I are both free. Well, at least I am. I owe her a great debt of gratitude."

When Buford was finished interviewing all of them, he asked them not to leave town. Betsy called for a taxi and the four of them left together, but the sheriff could feel the tension between them.

As he watched them leave, he wondered where the missing JJ was and why they all seemed to think she had killed Martin Sanderson.

BLYTHE KNEW SHE WAS TAKING a chance going home with this cowboy. But that's how she'd always lived her life. She was convinced that if she hadn't, she'd still be living in her mother's trailer in the middle of the desert with some abusive drunk like her mother had.

She had learned to take care of herself. She'd had to even before she'd left home at fourteen. There'd been too many nights when her mother would pass out and Blythe would hear the heavy footsteps of whatever boyfriend her mother had brought home from the bar coming down the hallway toward her room.

She'd been eleven when she started keeping a butcher knife under her pillow. She'd only had to use it once.

Blythe shoved that memory away as she watched the small Western town disappear behind them. The air was cooler now as Logan sped along the blacktop of a two-lane. The houses, she noted, were few and far between, and the farther they went, the less she saw of anything but open country.

The land ran green in rolling hills broken only occasionally by a tree or a rocky point. In one such tree, a bald eagle watched them pass. Several antelope stood silhouetted against a lush hillside. Further down, a handful of deer grazed on the new green grass. One lifted his head at the sound of the motorcycle. His ears were huge, reminding her of Mickey Mouse ears at Disney World.

Blythe stared at all the wild things they passed, having never seen them before except in magazines or on television.

As Logan turned onto a gravel road, slowing down a little, she saw cattle in the distance, dark against the horizon. Closer, a couple of horses loped along in the breeze.

When she looked up the road, she saw where the road ended. She really was out in the middle of nowhere. Alone with a man she'd didn't know. For all she knew, he could be more dangerous than what she'd left behind.

She could hear her mother's slurred words, the words she'd grown up with all those years ago.

"You think you're better than me?" The harsh cigarettes-and-booze laugh. "I can see your future, little girl. No matter how you try to fight it, you're headed for a bad end."

She *had* tried to fight it, and at one point, she'd actually thought she'd beaten her mother's prediction. But by then her mother was long dead and buried and there was no one there to hear her say, "See Mama, you were wrong. Look at your little girl now."

Blythe laughed softly. Wouldn't her mother love to be here now to see that all her predictions had come true. She would have been the first to tell her daughter that if you flew too high, too fast, you were headed for a fall.

Clearly, she'd proven that she had too much of her mother's blood in her. She'd flown high all right, but ultimately, it had caught up with her. She was now in free fall. And the worst part was, she knew she deserved it.

As Logan turned down an even smaller road, she stared at the stark landscape and wondered what she'd gotten herself into this time. Logan, she thought, must be thinking the same thing.

Maybe they were more alike than he thought.

The last of the day's sun had slipped below the horizon but not before painting the spring green rolling hills with gold. The sky, larger than any she'd ever seen, had turned to cobalt blue. Not even a cloud hung on the horizon.

At the end of the road, she caught a glimpse of an old farmhouse. Past it were an older barn and some horses in a pasture.

The house, she saw as they drew closer, had seen better days but she could tell it had recently been given a fresh coat of white paint. There was a porch with a couple of wooden chairs and curtains at the windows.

"It's not much," Logan said as he parked the motorcycle out front and they climbed off.

"It's great," she said meaning it. She couldn't see another house within miles. She'd never been in such an isolated place. Here she could pretend that she'd escaped her old life. At least for a little while.

As he opened the door, she noticed that he hadn't bothered to lock the house when he'd left. Trusting soul. She smiled at the thought. The kind of man who brought home a perfect stranger. Well, not perfect, far from it. But still a stranger.

BUFORD WAS GLAD TO HAVE turned the case over to the state crime techs. This would be a high-profile case and while he would still be involved, it was no longer solely on his shoulders.

It would be getting dark soon and he was anxious to get home for supper. He just hoped Clara would lay off the hot peppers. The woman was killing him.

Unfortunately, he couldn't quit thinking about the case, especially what might have been pinned to the man's robe. Too bad someone had taken the note.

He told himself the crime techs would be especially thorough on this one, since clearly Martin Sanderson was somebody. Not only did he own a place in the Grizzly Club, he was apparently some hotshot music producer from Los Angeles.

The club liked to play down the identities of their owners, how much money they had and how they made it. No need to announce it anyway, since the residents probably all knew much more about each other than any of the staff or people outside the club ever could. After all, if they had the dough to buy a place behind the gate, then they were instantly part of the club, weren't they? Clearly Kevin was merely staff.

Buford stopped at the guardhouse to ask about the woman visitor who'd at least said she was JJ when she'd picked up her key. He found it irritating that the residents who left the names of their guests didn't even want the guards to know exactly who was coming for a visit.

"These are people who have to be very careful," Kevin had said when Buford had questioned why they needed so much secrecy. "They worry that they could be kidnapped or their children kidnapped. They aren't like you and me."

"They die when they're shot in the heart just like you

and me," Buford pointed out and warranted himself a scowl from Kevin.

At the gate, the guard was more than glad to talk to the local sheriff about the guest allegedly known as JJ. He described a dark-haired good-looking woman. "She left in a hurry, I can tell you that. She barely waited for the gate to open."

"What was she driving?"

The guard described a silver sports car convertible. "I can give you her license plate number. We take those down on anyone coming or going."

Buford thanked him as he glanced at the plate number the guard gave him. It began with a 7, which meant a local Montana Lake County plate, probably a rental. "How did the woman seem to you when she left?"

"I didn't speak to her, barely got a glimpse of her."

"She was going *that* fast?" he asked in surprise since there were speed bumps near the gate.

"Well, she was moving at a good clip, but I was also about to check the guy on the motorcycle who was coming in just then."

"A club resident?"

He shook his head. "Not one I'd ever seen. But I didn't get a chance to talk to him. As I started toward him, he swung around and took off after the woman in the sports car."

"He *followed* her?"

The guard hesitated. "I saw him look at her as she left and then he seemed to go after her."

"He *knew* her?" Buford asked.

"I got the feeling he did."

"You didn't happen to get the plate on the motorcycle, did you?"

"No, but I'm sure our cameras caught it."

Buford waited. It didn't take long before the guard produced the bike plate number. He pocketed both, anxious to run them. But as he left the guard station his radio went off, alerting him of an accident on the road back to town.

A car had left the highway and crashed in the rocks at the edge of the lake. Firefighters and emergency medical services were on their way to the scene.

Buford turned on his flashing lights and siren. It was going to be a long night the way things were going.

As BLYTHE STEPPED INTO Logan's farmhouse, she wasn't sure what she would find. She half expected a woman's touch. She'd taken him for being about her own age, early thirties, which meant he could have been married at least once or at least lived with someone. But she was pleased to see that there was no sign that a woman had ever lived here.

"Like I said, basic," he noted almost apologetically.

"I like it. Simple is good." He had no idea how she'd been living.

She walked around, taking it in. The place was furnished with apparently the only thought to being practical and comfortable. There was an old leather couch in front of a small brick fireplace, an even older recliner next to it and a rug in front of the couch on the worn wooden floor. The kitchen had a 1950s metal and

Formica top table and four chairs. Through a door she spotted a bathroom and stairs that led up to the second floor, where she figured there would be bedrooms.

"Why don't I show you up to your room in case you want to freshen up," Logan said, shrugging out of his leather jacket.

She couldn't help noticing his broad shoulders, the well-formed chest, the slim hips, the incredibly long legs. It brought back the memory of being in his arms on the dance floor and sent a frisson of desire through her.

Logan headed up the stairs and she followed. Just as she'd figured, there were two bedrooms, one with a double bed, one with no furniture at all, and another bathroom, this one with a huge clawfoot tub.

One bed. She realized she hadn't thought out this part of her great escape. That was so like her. Not that the idea of sharing his bed hadn't crossed her mind. After all, she was the one who'd wanted to run away with him. What did she expect was going to happen?

He must have seen her expression. "You can have this room," he said motioning to the bed. "I'll take the couch."

"I don't want to take your bed."

He didn't give her a chance to argue the point. "I'll see what's in the fridge. Are you hungry? You didn't eat much at the last place we stopped. I could fry up some elk steaks."

She smiled, giving herself away. She couldn't explain this ravenous hunger she had except that maybe she was just tired of going to bed hungry and for all the wrong reasons.

"You've never had elk, right?"

"How did you know?" she said with a laugh.

"You're going to love it."

"I thought you raised *beef*," she said.

"I try to kill an elk every year or so. A little variety, you know?"

She thought she did know.

"There are towels in the cabinet in the bathroom. I just put clean sheets on the bed before I left. Holler if there is anything else you need," he said, and tromped back down the stairs, leaving her standing in his bedroom.

She glanced at the bed, tempted to lie down for a while. The ride here had taken five hours, which wasn't bad, but she hadn't slept well last night and for some time now she'd been running on fear-induced adrenaline.

The memory of what she had to fear sent a shaft of ice up her spine. She shivered even in the warm bedroom. The weight of her life choices pressed down on her chest and she had to struggle to breathe. Did she really think that she could escape the past—even in this remote part of Montana, even with this trusting cowboy?

"There's a price that comes with the life you've lived." Not her mother's voice this time. Martin Sanderson's. "And sweetheart, your bill has come due."

Chapter Four

The ambulance was there by the time Sheriff Buford Olson reached the accident scene. He parked along the edge of the narrow road where a highway patrolman was directing traffic. A wrecker was in the process of pulling the blackened car up from the rocky shore where it had landed, but he could still smell smoke.

As Buford walked to the edge of the road, he could see where the car had gone off, dropped over the steep edge of the road to tumble down the rocks before coming to a stop at the edge of the lake.

He noticed no skid marks on the pavement or in the dirt at the shoulder of the road. The driver hadn't even tried to brake before going off the road and over the rocky precipice?

"The passengers?" he asked as he spotted one of the ambulance drivers.

"Just one." The man shook his head.

Buford walked over to one of the highway patrolmen at the scene and asked if there was anything he could do to help.

"Pretty well have it covered," the officer said. "Looks like the driver was traveling at a high rate of speed when she missed the curve, plummeting over the edge of the road and rolling several times on the rocks before the car exploded."

Buford turned to watch the wrecker pull the car up from the edge of the lake, then asked to see the patrolman's report. He did a double take when he saw the license plate number the highway patrolman had put down.

He hurriedly pulled the slip of paper the security guard at the Grizzly Club had given him. It matched the sports car the woman guest had been driving earlier that morning.

"You get an ID when you ran the plate?" he asked the patrolman.

"The car was a rental. Rented under the name of Jennifer James yesterday."

JJ? Had to be, since the license plate was the same one the guard had given him.

As Buford left the scene, he couldn't help thinking how coincidental it was that one of Martin Sanderson's guests was now also dead. Of course, it could be that the woman had been killed because she was driving too fast away from the murder scene. That would have made a great theory if it hadn't been hours since she'd left the Grizzly Club driving too fast then too—before she'd apparently gone off the road and died at the edge of the lake.

So where had she been during those missing hours? The crash had occurred only miles from the Grizzly Club turnoff. And why hadn't she tried to brake?

Martin Sanderson had approved six guests. Jett

Atkins was accounted for and possibly JJ, along with three members of the all-girl band. Luca was apparently dead.

But it was the elusive JJ who captured his thoughts. That and the safety pin and missing note on Sanderson's robe.

Unfortunately, the woman who'd been driving this car was now on her way to the morgue and she might have been the only other person in the world who knew what that note said and why Martin Sanderson was dead.

LOGAN WENT DOWNSTAIRS AND dug some steaks out of the freezer. He had no idea what Blythe was doing here or what she was thinking. Or what she might be running from, but she was sure as the devil running from something.

He told himself it didn't matter, although he feared he could be wrong about that. Apparently the woman wanted a break from whatever life she'd been living. He didn't even know what that life had been or if he should be worried about it. But she triggered a powerful protective instinct in him that had made him throw caution to the wind.

Too bad she didn't trust him enough to tell him what was going on, he thought, then remembered the scrap of yellow paper he'd retrieved from under the booth table back at the café. He quickly reached into his pocket.

"Logan?"

He started at the sound of her voice directly behind him. It was the first time she'd said his name. It was like music off her tongue. His hand froze in his pocket as he turned.

"Would you mind if I took a bath?"

He withdrew his hand from his pocket sans the note and smiled. He'd seen the gleam in her eye when she'd spotted his big clawfoot tub. "You're in luck. There's even some bubble bath up there. A joke housewarming gift from my brothers."

"You have brothers?"

"Five."

She raised a brow. "Wow. Sisters?"

He shook his head. "Take as long as you want. I have steaks thawing for steak sandwiches later."

"Thanks." She started to turn away. "And thanks for bringing me here." With that she ran upstairs. A moment later he heard the water come on in the bathroom.

Thinking of her, he told himself there was something strong and carefree about this woman he'd brought home and, at the same time, vulnerable and almost fragile. Whatever she wanted or needed from him, he'd do his damnedest to give to her. Right now, though, it was just the use of his tub, he thought smiling, and tried not to imagine Blythe with her slim yet lush body up to her neck in bubbles.

He waited to make sure she didn't come back down before he withdrew the scrap of paper and pressed it open to see what was on it.

Logan wasn't sure what he'd expected to find on the piece of notepaper—if anything. He'd hoped it would be a clue to this woman.

He was disappointed.

There were only two words on the yellow note paper, both written in blue pen. *You're Next.*

He stared at them for a moment. Next for what? He had no idea. The words didn't offer any clue to Blythe, that was for sure. He wadded up the scrap of paper and tossed it into the garbage, pushing it down where it couldn't be seen. He felt foolish for retrieving it, worse for thinking it might be important.

CHARLIE BAKER LET OUT A STRING of profanity when he saw all the flashing lights on the highway ahead. Cops. The stupid woman had gotten pulled over for speeding.

He swore again as his line of traffic came to a dead stop and he saw a highway patrolman walking down the line of cars toward him. Realizing regrettably that he had no way of getting out of the traffic, he quickly checked himself in his rearview mirror.

Charlie and his girlfriend had been on the road from Arizona for four days. He knew he looked rough. Hopefully not so rough that the officer would run the plates on this stolen pickup, especially with a warrant already out on him.

As the cop neared, Charlie put his window down, wishing he hadn't listened to Susie. Earlier he'd stopped to take a leak beside the road. It had been her idea to take that sports car after she'd found the keys on the floorboard—and the purse lying on the passenger seat.

He had looked around, pretty sure that whoever it

belonged to had walked down to the lake and would be coming back any minute. They'd argued about taking the car, but Susie said the owner deserved to have it stolen—hell, was *asking* to have it stolen.

Once she opened the glove box and realized it was a rental, there had been no more argument. "I'm taking it. It might be my only chance to drive a car like this and it sure as hell beats that old pickup you *borrowed*."

She'd been bitching about the vehicle he'd stolen since they left Arizona and he'd been getting real tired of it.

"We can dump the pickup," she'd said. "It's probably going to break down soon anyway."

"We'll talk about it away from here," he'd said. There was something about this that made him uneasy. Who just left such an expensive car beside the road with the keys and a purse in it?

But there was no arguing with Susie. She got in the car and started it up, revving the engine too loud.

Charlie hadn't wanted to be around when whoever had rented the car came racing up and found Susie behind the wheel. He'd taken off in the pickup, yelling at her that he'd meet her down the road at the campground where they'd spent last night.

Only she hadn't shown. Back at the camp, he'd fallen asleep and lost track of time. Susie should have shown hours ago. He figured she'd probably taken off in that convertible and left him high and dry. But he'd decided he'd better go look for her, since if she was in trouble, he knew she'd rat him out in a heartbeat, and now here he was with a cop heading for him.

The officer stepped to his window. "There's been an accident. It could be a little bit before we get the road cleared."

That damned Susie had gone on a joyride and left him. Or, he realized, she could be caught in the traffic on the other side of the wreck just like he was. "What kind of accident, officer?"

"A car went off the road." He was already walking away.

Charlie watched him head down the highway to tell the other drivers of cars piling up behind him. Or, he thought, Susie might have wrecked that convertible. With a curse, he waited a minute before he got out of the pickup and worked his way along the edge of the trees to where a few people had gathered on the side of the road.

It was almost too dark to see what was going on, but as he drew closer, he smelled smoke. Joining the others gawking at the scene, he saw what was left of the pretty silver sports car convertible that Susie just had to drive being lifted up onto the back of a wrecker's flatbed.

"Did the driver get out?" he asked the man standing next to him.

"Trapped in the car. I heard the EMT say she was burned beyond recognition."

As Charlie turned to walk back to his pickup, he took an inventory of his emotions, surprised how little he felt other than anger. He should have known Susie wouldn't know how to drive a car like that. *He* should have driven it. Served her right.

But he knew if he had taken the car, he wouldn't have met Susie at the campground. He would have just kept going, leaving her and the stolen pickup behind. Susie probably knew that, he thought as he climbed into the truck and waited for the highway to clear so he could get the hell out of this state.

He had been getting real tired of Susie anyway. Fortunately, he'd insisted on taking everything from the purse she'd found in that expensive convertible. The cash and credit cards were going to come in handy.

Charlie smiled to himself. He'd never had good luck, but sometimes things had a way of working out for the best, didn't they.

BUFORD HAD TO STOP BY HIS office on the way home and was shocked that he had a half-dozen calls from reporters. As tight-lipped as the Grizzly Club was, he couldn't believe word had gotten out this quickly. But people liked to talk—especially when it was something juicy like the death of a wealthy man from the Grizzly Club. And he'd already caught Jett on his phone.

He decided to see how bad it was. He picked up one of the messages and dialed the number.

"Is it true that JJ was killed tonight on the road just outside of Big Fork?" the reporter asked.

Not about Martin Sanderson? "I'm sorry but I can't…" He realized she'd called the victim JJ. "The accident is under investigation." He hung up frowning.

Who would have given a reporter that information? No one at the scene, even if they'd overheard that the car had been rented to a Jennifer James. Who knew that Jennifer James was known as JJ?

Jett, he'd bet on it. Buford had insisted on the cell phone numbers of Jett and the three members of the former band in case he needed to ask them any more questions. He'd warned all of them not to leave town until the investigation was complete.

None of them had been happy about the prospect of staying around, since they couldn't stay at the Grizzly Club and had been forced to take a cheap motel instead. Betsy had called him to tell him where they were staying, as per his request.

As he grabbed his phone to call, Buford felt his stomach rumble. He was starved. He'd picked up a couple of cheeseburgers at a fast-food restaurant on his way back to his office. Clara would kill him. He was supposed to be on a diet. But she was killing him anyway with those darned chili peppers. He'd prefer to drop dead after eating a cheeseburger any day than keep living with his belly on fire.

He dialed the cell phone number Jett had given him. Jett answered on the third ring and didn't sound all that happy about hearing from him so soon.

"I just had a reporter call me," Buford said. "You didn't happen to—"

"I haven't talked to anyone."

Maybe. Maybe not. From what he'd seen of his granddaughter's rock 'n' roll idol, Jett liked publicity and he didn't seem to care if it was good or bad. He'd talk to anyone, even the tabloids, and he'd admitted that he let Martin use him and JJ for publicity stunts.

"What about the others?"

"Nope," Jett said after getting confirmation from the three women. Buford could hear the background noises. Apparently they were all in a restaurant together.

"Not even about the accident?" Buford said.

"*Accident?* Is that what you're calling it?" Jett snapped. "I should have known JJ would get away with this. She's always gotten away with whatever she did. Have you found her? Is that what she claims? That she *accidentally* killed Martin?"

So he didn't know about the car wreck. Which meant neither did the others, and they couldn't have called the press. But they were certainly quick to blame JJ for murder even before all the facts were in.

Buford decided to let Jett and the women read about the wreck in the morning papers. "I'll let you finish your supper then. Wait, one more question. Why did JJ want out of her contract?"

Jett sighed. "You really don't know much about the music business, do you? Martin discovered JJ, took over her career, made her a star. She wanted more control over her career and her life, but she was making him a ton of money. He would never have let her go though. She knew that."

"Does she also go by the name of Jennifer James?" He asked the real question he had wanted to ask, hoping to confirm what he *did* know.

"*Yes,*" Jett said impatiently, as if everyone knew that. "Is that all?"

"For now," he said and hung up.

He started to call it a night. But then he remembered

the man on the motorcycle that the guard thought had chased after the infamous JJ.

When he ran the number, Buford got a surprise.

LOGAN HAD THE STEAKS COOKED and everything ready for a late supper when Blythe came down wearing his robe and smelling of lilac bubble bath. Her wet, long, dark hair was pulled up on top of her head and he was struck by how beautiful she looked. Everything about her took his breath away. As little as he knew about her, he felt they were kindred souls somehow.

"Tell me about this part of Montana," she said as they ate. It was dark outside, the sky filled with millions of sparkling stars and a sliver of silver moon. A breeze stirred the curtains at the kitchen window. The house felt almost cozy.

He told her about the outlaw era that brought such infamous luminaries as Kid Curry, Butch Cassidy and the Sundance Kid to the area. "It was the last lawless place in Montana."

He told her how the railroad had come through and brought settlers who were given land and a time limit on improving the acres if they wanted to keep it.

"It was a hard place to survive. Not many of them made it. You had to be hardy."

"Like your family?" she asked.

He smiled at that. "Chisholm roots run deep, that's for sure." He didn't tell her how his ancestors had brought up a herd of cattle from Texas and each generation had helped build up Chisholm Cattle Company to what it was today.

Longhorns hadn't done well because of the tough winters. Once they'd changed to Black Angus cattle, the ranch had thrived.

"I saw the horses out in the pasture," she said. "Are they yours?"

"Do you ride?"

She laughed and shook her head. "But I've always wanted to."

"Tomorrow I'll teach you," he said on impulse.

"Really?" She looked excited about the prospect. There was a peacefulness to her that he hadn't seen since they were on the dance floor last night.

"I think you'll like it, and when you're ready, I'll show you more of my part of Montana by horseback."

"I'd love that," she said and finished her sandwich.

"You liked the elk?" he asked amused at the way she ate. He had joked that she acted as if she wasn't sure where her next meal might be coming from, but now wondered if that wasn't the case. She'd said that the sports car she'd been driving didn't belong to her. For all he knew, she might not have anything more than the clothes on her back.

Maybe she *had* been a guest at the Grizzly Club, but he had a bad feeling he'd been right and she'd borrowed a car she shouldn't have.

He shook his head at the thought that he might be harboring a criminal. And such a beautiful, engaging one at that.

As they finished the elk steaks, Logan looked across the table at his guest and saw how exhausted she was. He felt a strange contentment being here with her like this. It surprised him. He never brought any of his dates back to his house. But then this woman wasn't exactly a date, was she?

"There's a quilt up on the bed that my great grandmother made," he said. "You look like you're ready to crawl under it."

She smiled, appearing almost as content as he felt.

He got up and cleared the dishes, putting them in the sink, then he went to the closet and pulled down the extra blankets he kept there. Winters in this old farmhouse were downright cold, and there were many nights when he'd fallen asleep in front of the fire—the only really warm place in the house.

Dropping them on the couch, he turned to find her standing in the kitchen doorway. "Don't you want me to help you with the dishes?" She looked cute wearing his robe. He watched her pull it around her, hugging herself as if even the spring night felt cold to her. It slid over her curves in a way that made him realize he would never look at that robe the same way again.

"The dishes can wait. Why don't you get some sleep? I'll saddle up the horses in the morning and we'll get you ridin'."

She seemed to hesitate for a moment, then smiled gratefully. "Thank you. For everything."

He nodded. "It's nice to have you here." It was true, but still he hadn't meant to say it, let alone admit it. He'd never been without female company if he'd wanted it. But he often found women confusing. He preferred his horse.

Not this woman, though.

Even after she went upstairs, he could smell lilac and felt a stirring in him at the mere thought of her. He'd felt drawn to her from that moment he'd seen her expression on the dance floor. He recalled the way she had moved to the music.

As he heard her close his bedroom door, he groaned to himself. He must be losing his grip. His brothers would think him a damned fool. Not just for bringing a woman he knew nothing about back to his house, but for letting such a beautiful woman go to bed alone— and in his bed.

Whatever her reason for being here, it wasn't because she couldn't resist him, he thought with a laugh. Logan Chisholm wasn't used to that, either.

As he lay down on the couch and pulled a blanket over him, he told himself she would be gone in the morning—and probably with his pickup and any cash she could find.

But as he heard her moving around upstairs, he found himself smiling. He could always get another truck.

Chapter Five

The motorcycle that the guard at the Grizzly Club said had gone after the woman in the silver sports car was registered to Logan Chisholm, the address Chisholm Cattle Company, Whitehorse, Montana.

Sheriff Buford Olson let out a low whistle. Hoyt Chisholm was one of the wealthiest ranchers in the state, so it was no surprise his son might be visiting the Grizzly Club. Or even that he might know the woman who'd been visiting Martin Sanderson, as the guard had suggested.

So what had he been doing on this side of the Rockies? Visiting his friend JJ? Did that mean that Logan Chisholm also knew Martin Sanderson?

Buford picked up the phone. His stomach growled again and he noticed how late it was. He'd call him tomorrow. Probably a waste of time anyway, since Logan Chisholm hadn't actually gone into the Grizzly Club.

But Chisholm had seen Jennifer James leaving and possibly followed her. He might know where she'd gone between the time she was seen leaving the club and going out in a blaze that evening beside Flathead Lake.

Sighing, Buford put the phone back. He was starved

and it was late. Also, he didn't relish telling Logan Chisholm about the dead woman—that was if Logan even knew this JJ. Chisholm was probably still in the Bigfork area, which meant he would read about it in the papers.

There was always the chance that if Chisholm knew something about either death, he would come forward with any information he had. Buford had never heard much about Hoyt Chisholm's sons except that they were adopted and there were a bunch of them. Which meant they hadn't been in too much trouble. With a father as well known as Hoyt Chisholm, it would be hard to stay out of the headlines if the sons had run-ins with the law. Even Chisholm's money could only do so much when it came to the press.

It certainly hadn't been able to keep Hoyt's name out of the headlines when he'd lost first one wife, then another. The first wife had drowned, the second had been killed in a horseback riding accident, the third had disappeared, recently turning up dead, murdered.

Buford had followed the case with interest. Hoyt had been arrested, but later cleared. An insurance investigator by the name of Agatha Wells had been arrested for the third wife's murder. Last Buford had heard, Agatha Wells had been sent to the state mental hospital for evaluation and had escaped.

It had been nasty business, since Hoyt Chisholm had recently taken a fourth wife, Emma. The insurance investigator had come after her as well, abducting her at one point. Later Agatha Wells was believed to have drowned in the Milk River after being shot by a sheriff's deputy on the Chisholm ranch. Her body, though, had never been found.

He hoped Logan Chisholm didn't have any connection to Martin Sanderson's death. The Chisholm family had been through enough.

Picking up his hat, Buford pushed himself up out of his chair. He'd spent too much time on his feet today and he ached all over. As he turned out his office light, all he could think about was his big leather recliner waiting for him in front of the television. He had a lot on his mind. And he couldn't quit thinking about that note that had been pinned to Martin Sanderson's body. He'd give anything to know what it said. He had a feeling it would solve this case.

So much about the case nagged at him. Why had Martin Sanderson invited all of the members of the former Tough as Nails band to Montana and left keys for them when he had to know that the one called Luca was dead?

And what, if anything, did this Jennifer James, JJ, have to do with it?

It wasn't until he got home to discover his granddaughter visiting that he found out just who JJ had been.

BETSY HARPER GLANCED AROUND the table in the motel restaurant dining room, marveling at how little they had all changed. Loretta was still brassy, loud and demanding. Karen had always been quiet, never letting anyone know what she was thinking.

And Jett was Jett, she thought with no small amount

of bitterness. He had barely acknowledged her, but what did she expect? He'd dumped her for JJ ten years ago and done her a favor in retrospect.

He would have made a lousy husband, an even worse father. Still, he'd been her first, and she somehow thought that might have made a difference to him. Apparently, it didn't.

"So what do you think of this whole mess?" Jett asked after he'd joined them in the motel restaurant dining room.

They'd decided to all stay at the same motel. Jett had joked about keeping enemies close. Betsy supposed that was how he felt. Just like JJ, he'd definitely betrayed them all, some of them more than others.

Conversation had been stilted. Loretta had gone on for a while complaining about how bad her life was. As if they couldn't just look at her and see that she was hard up for money. Loretta blamed Martin and was convinced Tough as Nails could have been great if he hadn't broken up the band.

"I'm not sorry Martin's dead," Loretta said now. "I just wish I'd shot him."

"Who says you didn't?" Jett said. "We all think it was JJ, but maybe she didn't do it."

"I think she did it," Betsy said. "Why else would she take off the way she did?" Jett had told them that JJ had been staying in a wing of the main house and that he'd seen her prints in Martin's blood—and so had the sheriff.

"Maybe she ran to avoid *us*," Karen said without looking up from her meal. "If like you said Martin was threatening her with this reunion tour… She was probably afraid that we all hated her."

Jett laughed. "Like you don't. I would have loved to have seen her face when she found out what Martin was up to. I'm surprised she didn't kill him with her bare hands."

"I can't believe she agreed to a reunion tour," Betsy said.

Karen gave her a you-can't-be-that-naïve look. None of them knew just how naïve she'd always been about a lot of things.

"Jett just said JJ knew nothing about it," Karen said impatiently to her. "There was never going to be a tour. It was just Martin messing with us again."

"Well, he's dead now." Jett waved the waiter over. "Anyone else want to drink to that? I'm in the mood to celebrate. Champagne," he told the waiter.

"You're the only one who thinks this is a celebration," Karen said. "A man has been murdered and you're all ready to string JJ up for it."

"Well, if one of *us* didn't kill him, then who else was there?" Jett said. "We're the only ones who had motive, opportunity and means, since there was a handgun on the floor beside him. I heard the sheriff check. It belonged to Martin."

"But JJ is the only one missing, isn't she?" Loretta pointed out.

The waiter brought the champagne and glasses. Jett poured himself a glass and lifted it for a toast. "Here's to JJ, wherever she might be. If she was here I would thank her."

No one else reached for a glass, but that didn't keep Jett from emptying his.

As he set his down, his gaze settled on Betsy. She felt the heat of his look as he asked, "What do you girls have planned to amuse yourselves until we can get out of this godforsaken place?"

KAREN FELT DISGUSTED BEING around Jett again. She hated that they were all acting as if nothing had happened ten years ago.

Betsy was the worst. Jett had broken her heart. Karen remembered how despondent she'd been. She'd had to hold Betsy's hand through that horrible time while keeping her own pain and anger to herself.

Now as she watched Jett turning his charm on Betsy, she wanted to throw something at him. Throw something at Betsy, too. Hadn't the woman learned what a no-count Jett was? He used people, then discarded them. One look at Jett and Betsy should have known the man hadn't changed.

"I, for one, am going to turn in early," Karen said tossing down her napkin and rising. "I regret ever coming here."

"You came because you felt like you owed us," Loretta said snidely.

Karen turned on her. "It wasn't your guilt trip that made me change my mind and come after you pleaded with me," she snapped. "I did it because I got tired of listening to you whine."

"Now, ladies," Jett said.

"There are no ladies here," Loretta said with a laugh.

"I think I *will* have a drink, Jett. That is, if you're buying." She picked up one of the champagne glasses and held it out. He happily filled it.

"I didn't want to come, either," Betsy said. "But I also didn't want to be the one band member who ruined it for the others."

"How could we have had a reunion tour without Luca anyway?" Karen said.

"Bands do tours all the time without the original members," Jett said.

"There wasn't going to be a reunion tour," Karen snapped as she started to step away from the table.

"Then why get us here?" Betsy said, sounding surprised and disheartened.

Karen was tired of Betsy's apparent naïveté. No one could be that sweet and innocent, she thought as she walked away.

Behind her, she heard Jett say, "I think he was hoping one of you would kill JJ."

Loretta's laugh and words followed Karen out of the room. "What makes you think we didn't?"

EMMA CHISHOLM STOOD AT THE window looking out at the rolling prairie. Chisholm land as far as the eye could see. She'd fallen in love with this place, the same way she had with Hoyt Chisholm, only months ago.

Of course, she hadn't had any idea what was in store for her when she'd agreed down in Denver to run off with him to Vegas for a quickie marriage. They hadn't known each other. They hadn't cared. Love does that to you. He'd told her the ranch was large and isolated.

"Sounds wonderful," she'd said, and he'd laughed.

"Some women can't take that kind of emptiness."

"I'm not some women." But she'd heard the pain in his voice and known there had been others before her who he'd taken back to the ranch. All she'd known then was that they hadn't lasted. A man in his late fifties would have had at least a wife or maybe even two, she'd thought then.

It wasn't until she'd come to Whitehorse, Montana, and met Aggie Wells that she'd found out she'd underestimated Hoyt's history with wives—and pain. He'd been married three other times, all three ending tragically, as it turned out.

Former insurance investigator Aggie Wells had brought the news along with a warning that Emma was next. "He killed his other wives. I can't prove it," Aggie had said, "but I keep trying. Watch yourself."

Emma hadn't believed it. She knew Hoyt soul deep, as they say. He wasn't a killer. She'd just assumed like everyone else that Aggie was either obsessed with her husband—or just plain crazy.

That was months ago, she thought now as she looked out across the land and realized she'd been living with ghosts—the ghosts of her husband's exes and now Aggie's ghost.

So why did she still expect to see one of them coming across the prairie with only one goal in mind, killing her, the fourth and no doubt final wife of Hoyt Chisholm?

No one knew about the ghosts she'd been living with.

As much as she and her husband shared, she couldn't share these thoughts with Hoyt.

"Aggie Wells is dead," Hoyt had said. "She was shot. You saw her fall into the river. She didn't come up."

But when the sheriff had dragged the river, they hadn't found her body.

"She got hung up on something, a root, a limb, an old barbed-wire fence downriver," Hoyt said. "When the river goes down this summer, we'll find her body. But until then, she's gone, okay?"

But it hadn't been okay, because Emma had come to know Aggie, had actually liked her, maybe worse had believed in her heart that the woman might not be crazy. Nor dead. If anyone could survive being shot and even drowned, it would be Aggie.

The insurance investigator wasn't the only ghost Emma now lived with, though. Hoyt's first wife, Laura Chisholm, was the ghost that caused her sleepless night. Aggie had come to believe Laura hadn't drowned that day on Fort Peck Reservoir but was still alive and vengefully killing Hoyt's wives.

Aggie had even provided photographs of a woman who looked so much like what Laura Chisholm would look like now after all these years that it had made Hoyt pale. Seeing the effect the photographs had on her husband had made a believer out of Emma. And if you believed Laura Chisholm was alive, then you also had to believe that she had murdered not one but possibly all of Hoyt's other wives—and would eventually come for Emma herself, like the living ghost she was.

Hoyt didn't believe it. At least that's what he said.

But if that were true, then why would he continue to insist on someone hanging around near the ranch house so Emma was never left alone?

She laughed softly at a thought. Didn't Hoyt realize that she was never really alone? Either Aggie's ghost or Laura's was always with her—at least in her thoughts. She was merely waiting for one of the ghosts to appear. Either Aggie trying to save her again or Laura determined to kill her.

"What are you baking?" Hoyt asked as he came into the kitchen and pulled her from her thoughts.

"Gingersnaps," she said, stepping away from the window and back to her baking. Baking was the one thing that took her mind off the waiting. She was always baking or cooking or cleaning. Hiring help had proved to be difficult after all the trouble here on the ranch. Suspicion hung over the place like thick smoke.

"I hate seeing you work so much," Hoyt said now. "I've called an agency in Billings. We have that guestroom at the far wing. What would you think about live-in help? No one wants to drive all the way out here from Whitehorse. I think this will work better."

She didn't correct him. It wasn't the drive and he knew it. Maybe people in Billings didn't know about the Chisholm Curse, as it was called.

"I don't need any help. You know I like to keep busy," Emma said, but she could tell he was determined to hire someone. Normally she would have put up a fight, but the truth was, having someone living in the house and helping sounded like a blessing. That way

Hoyt and his sons could go back to running this ranch instead of babysitting her.

Hoyt came up behind her, put his arms around her and pulled her close. She closed her eyes and leaned back into him. Never had she felt such love.

"Dawson just left for home," her husband said, nuzzling her neck. Her stepson Dawson had been assigned to Emma duty that day, which meant he'd spent the day pretending he had things to do around the ranch's main house and yard. Did any of them really believe they were fooling her?

Certainly not Hoyt, she thought as she turned off the mixer and let him lead her upstairs to their bedroom. The cookies could wait. Being in her husband's strong arms could not.

She knew as he closed the bedroom door that he believed their love was like a shield that would protect them. She prayed he was right, but alive or dead, his first wife and Aggie Wells were anything but gone for good.

FORMER INSURANCE INVESTIGATOR Aggie Wells had come close to dying. She still wasn't her old self. For months, she'd felt her strength seep out of her and now wondered if she would ever be the same again.

She told herself she was lucky to be alive. If the bullet had been a quarter of an inch one way or the other it would have nicked a vital organ and she would have drowned in that creek.

It surprised her that she'd survived against all odds. How easy it would have been to give in to death. She still had nightmares remembering how long she'd had to stay underwater to avoid the sheriff's deputies catching her.

That memory always came with the bitter bite of betrayal. She'd trusted Emma Chisholm. That stupid, stupid woman. Aggie had been trying to save her life and what did she get for it? Shot and almost drowned.

In her more charitable moments, she reminded herself that she *had* abducted Emma just months before that day on the river. Still, she'd risked capture to bring Emma important information about Laura Chisholm.

Also, Emma had seemed as surprised as Aggie had that day when they'd heard the sheriff and her deputies coming through the trees. Maybe Emma hadn't informed them about the meeting by the river. At least that's what Aggie liked to believe. She liked Emma and now there was nothing she could do to save her. *The die is cast,* she thought. After surviving the cold water and the bullet wound, Aggie had gotten pneumonia and barely survived.

Her weight had dropped drastically and she didn't seem to have any strength to fight it. She told herself she was bouncing back, but a part of her knew it wasn't true. Worse, she feared she would never see this case through.

A small, bitter laugh escaped her lips. It wasn't her case, hadn't been for years. The insurance company she'd worked for had fired her because she hadn't been able to let the Chisholm case go.

She couldn't really blame them. She'd gotten it all wrong anyway. When Hoyt Chisholm's first wife,

Laura, had allegedly drowned in Fort Peck Reservoir, Aggie had been convinced Hoyt had killed her.

He'd remarried not long after. He had adopted six sons who needed homes, and if any man was desperate for a wife, it would have been him. Tasha Chisholm had been killed in a horseback-riding accident.

Aggie couldn't believe he'd kill another one. And then along came Krystal. Did he really think he could get away with a third murder?

Krystal Chisholm had disappeared not long into the marriage. By then Aggie had been pulled off the case, but that hadn't stopped her. She couldn't let him get away with killing another wife.

The first two deaths appeared to be accidents—at least to the unsuspecting. The third wife's disappearance could never be proved to be anything more than that.

"But I knew better," Aggie said to herself. Her faint voice echoed in the small room of what had once been a motel and was now a cheap studio apartment where she'd been hiding on the south side of Billings.

She'd hit a brick wall in her covert investigation back then. The insurance company had warned her off the case. But eventually they found out and fired her.

Fortunately, she'd saved every dime she'd ever made, so money wasn't a problem. She'd taken on private investigations when she felt like it. She was good at what she did, putting herself in someone else's shoes until she knew them inside and out.

Thankfully, she'd helped people who, when called

on, couldn't say no to helping her. Like the surgeon she'd had to call after she was shot.

She might have given up the Chisholm cases—if Hoyt Chisholm hadn't married a fourth time all these years later. Aggie had no choice but to warn Emma Chisholm. The woman was blind in love.

"Just as you had no choice but to abduct her once you figured out who the murderer really was," Aggie said to the empty room, then pulled herself up some in the threadbare recliner where she sat.

Only a little sun spilled in through the dirty window between the two frayed and faded curtains. The light bothered her now. Her illness had seemed to affect her eyes. She drew her attention away from the crack in the curtains, feeling too weak to get up and close them tighter.

But no one believed her. Instead, law enforcement was convinced that Aggie herself had killed Hoyt's second and third wives in an attempt to frame him for murder.

She scoffed at that. This was about obsession. Not Aggie's with this case, but Laura's with Hoyt. Aggie understood obsession, she knew how it could take over your life.

If only the sheriff had listened to her. Instead, she'd been arrested and sent to the state mental hospital for evaluation. They thought *she* was crazy?

Aggie smiled to herself as she remembered how she'd slipped through the cracks, sending another woman to the state mental hospital who actually needed the help.

Her smile faded quickly though as she reminded herself that she had failed. That day beside the river she had brought Emma the proof that Laura Chisholm was alive and living just hours away in Billings as a woman named Sharon Jones.

But when she'd come out of her fever, surfacing again at death's door, she'd asked the doctor if a woman named Sharon Jones had been arrested.

"I had hoped and yet I knew better," she said to herself. Laura was like a warm breeze in summer, drifting in and out unnoticed. She had to be to stay hidden all these years, appearing only to kill and then disappear again.

The doctor had given her the bad news. Sharon Jones hadn't been arrested and now she'd disappeared again. "I went by the house you asked me to check," the doctor told her. "It was empty. No sign of anyone."

Laura Chisholm was still on the loose. She would take another identity and when the time was right, she would strike again. Emma Chisholm was going to die and there wasn't anything Aggie could do about it.

Chapter Six

It was late by the time Logan headed for the barn to saddle his horse the next day. He must have been more tired than he'd thought. He couldn't remember sleeping this late in the day since college.

Once saddled, he rode down the half-mile lane to pick up his mail from the box on the county road. As much as he loved being on the back of his motorcycle, he loved being on the back of a horse just as much.

It was a beautiful Montana spring day, the sky a brilliant blue, no clouds on the horizon and the sun spreading warmth over the vibrant green land. He loved this time of year, loved the smells, the feel of new beginnings.

He wondered if that was what his houseguest was looking for. She'd apparently bailed—at least for a while—on her old life, whatever that was. He hadn't slept all that well last night knowing she was upstairs. And this morning he had no more idea what she was all about than he had when he'd met her the other night at the bar. He hadn't heard a sound out of her by the time he'd left. For all he knew she'd sneaked out last night and was long gone.

At least she hadn't taken his pickup.

He'd already decided to take a few days off work and, if she hadn't bailed on him as well, show her his part of Montana if she was still up for it. But then what, he wondered? Eventually, he had to get back to work. His father and brothers would be wondering what was going on. The last thing he needed was for one of them to show up at the house, he thought as he reached the county road.

Logan realized Blythe didn't really know who he was, either. He felt almost guilty about that—even though she had been anything but forthcoming about herself. He wanted her to like him for himself and not for his family money. Of course, it could be that she already knew who he was—knew that night at the bar when he'd asked her to dance. His family had certainly been in the news enough with that mess about Aggie Wells.

He pushed away the memory, just glad that it was over. With Aggie Wells dead, that should be the end of speculation about his father's other wives' deaths.

Logan thought instead of Blythe and his reservations about her. He recalled her new cowboy boots. She wouldn't be the first woman who'd come to Montana to meet herself a cowboy. Even better a rich one.

But with a self-deprecating grin, he reminded himself that she hadn't even made a play for him. Maybe that was the plan, since it seemed to be working. He couldn't get her off his mind.

Swinging down from the horse, he collected his mail and the newspapers that had stacked up since he'd been gone. He glanced at today's *Great Falls Tribune,* scanning the headlines before stuffing everything into one of his saddlebags, climbing back into the saddle and heading home.

As he rode up to the house, he saw her come out onto the porch.

"Good morning," he called to her as he dismounted, relieved she hadn't taken off. Even without his pickup. "Out for a morning ride?"

"Just went down to get the mail and my newspapers," he said as he dug them out of the saddlebag. "You up for a ride?"

She eyed the horse for a moment. "Do you have a shorter horse?"

He chuckled as he turned toward her. "I have a nice gentle one just for you." He noticed that she was wearing one of his shirts. It looked darned good on her. "Want to ride or have something to eat first?"

"Ride."

Logan knew he would have granted her anything she wanted at that moment. She was beautiful in an understated way that he found completely alluring. Her face, free of makeup, shone. There was a freshness about her that reminded him of the spring morning. She seemed relaxed and happy, her good mood contagious.

"Let's get you saddled up, then," he said, and led her out to the barn.

"This isn't going to be like a rodeo, is it?"

He laughed. "No bucking broncos, I promise. Don't worry, you're in good hands."

He showed her how to saddle her horse, then led it outside and helped her climb on.

"I like the view from up here," Blythe said, smiling down from the saddle. "So what do I do now?"

He gave her some of the basics, then climbed on his own horse. At first he just rode her around the pasture, but she was such a natural, he decided to show her a little piece of the ranch.

"This is what you do every day?" she asked, sounding awed.

He laughed. "It's a little more than a ride around the yard."

"You said you chase cows." She glanced around. "So where are these cows?"

"They're still in winter pasture. We'll be taking them up into the mountains pretty soon."

"You and your brothers. You ranch together?"

Her horse began to trot back toward the barn, saving him from answering. He rode alongside her, giving her pointers. She had great balance. It surprised him how quickly she'd caught on, and he wondered if she really had never ridden before.

"You're a natural," he said when they reached the house. It was late afternoon. They'd ridden farther than he'd originally planned, but it had been so enjoyable he hadn't wanted to return to the house.

"I had so much fun," she said as she swung down out of the saddle. "I wish we could do it again tomorrow." She groaned, though, and he could tell she was feeling the long ride.

"We can do it again tomorrow, if you're up to it," he said, liking the idea of another day with her.

"You probably need to start chasing cows again and I should be taking off, though, huh?" She looked away when she said it.

He really needed to get back to work, but he said, "I can take a few days off." As she helped him unsaddle the horses and put the tack away, he wondered again how long she planned to stay and where, if anywhere, the two of them were headed.

He knew he wouldn't be able to keep his family from Blythe long. Since his father Hoyt had remarried after years of raising his six sons alone, all six sons were expected to be at supper each evening. His stepmother Emma wanted them to spend time together as a family, and she was a great cook. It was just a matter of time before the family heard he was back and started wondering why he hadn't been around.

LORETTA WAS WAITING FOR THE others late the next morning down in the coffee shop. She'd already had a cup of coffee, which had only managed to make her more jittery. How long was the sheriff going to keep them here? She was broke and wondering how she was going to pay her motel bill, let alone eat.

Not to mention the latest news she'd just heard before coming down to the coffee shop. JJ had been killed yesterday in a car accident.

As Betsy and Karen joined her, she said, "You heard?"

"It's on all the news stations," Karen said.

"You and JJ had been closer than the rest of us," Loretta said, noticing that Karen had been crying.

"They were best friends when they were kids, huh," Betsy said.

That was news to Loretta.

"We grew up next door to each other," Karen said. "People thought we were sisters." She smiled at the memory, her eyes filling with tears.

"Must have been hard when she left the band," Loretta said. "So did she keep in touch with you?"

"No." Karen looked away.

"I thought it was just us," Betsy said. "But then none of us kept in touch either after that first year. Not surprising, I guess."

"Yeah, after everything that happened," Loretta agreed. She'd called Betsy a couple of times but felt like she'd gotten the cold shoulder. Karen, who she thought always acted as if she thought she was better than everyone, she hadn't even bothered to call.

"So we know what Betsy's been doing the last ten years, cranking out kids," Loretta said. "What about you, Karen?"

"I work in New York as a magazine editor."

Beat the hell out of Loretta's bartending job and part-time drumming gigs.

"So you never married?" Betsy asked.

"Three times. None of them stuck," Loretta said. "What about you, Karen?"

Karen shook her head.

"You got married quick enough after the band split," Loretta said to Betsy. "But I get the feeling you're still carrying a torch for Jett." Loretta couldn't help herself, even though Karen shot her a warning look.

"Jett made the rounds among us," Karen said pointedly, "but I don't think any of us were ever serious about him."

"Is that right?" Jett said shoving Karen over as he joined them in the booth.

Loretta didn't miss the look Jett and Betsy exchanged. He was up to his old tricks, she thought, and wondered what Betsy's husband would have to say about it. That was, if anyone bothered to tell him.

She discarded the idea. What did she care? She hadn't come here to bond with her former band members. She'd come for the money and now there wasn't any.

"You all heard about JJ?" Jett said, glancing around the table. He looked solemn for a moment before he asked with a grin, "So which one of you killed her?"

"Why would any of us want to kill JJ?" Karen asked with obvious annoyance.

Jett shrugged. "Jealousy. I've already told the sheriff to check the brakes on her rental car."

"Jealous? Not over you," Loretta said.

"Maybe," he said still grinning. "But I definitely felt some professional jealousy. JJ became a star while the rest of you—"

"Did just fine," Karen said. "Let's not forget that JJ, according to the tabloids, had been trying to get out of her contract. I don't think her life was a bed of roses."

"So we're all supposed to feel sorry for her?" Loretta asked. "Excuse me, but she dumped us. Sold us right down the river. I, for one, haven't forgotten or forgiven." When she saw the way everyone was staring at her, she added, "But I had nothing to do with her driving her car off a cliff."

"I'm sure it was just an accident," Betsy said.

"Sure," Jett replied with a chuckle. "Just like Martin getting shot through the heart."

BUFORD'S PHONE HAD BEEN ringing off the hook all day. As hard as Kevin had tried to keep the news of Martin Sanderson's death from the media, he'd failed.

"Mr. Sanderson's death is under investigation," the sheriff said. "That's all I can tell you at this time."

When his phone rang yet again, he'd snatched it up, expecting it would be another reporter.

"You knew about JJ's accident last night," Jett Atkins said the moment Buford picked up.

He recognized his voice but said, "I'm sorry, who is this?"

"Jett Atkins. You knew JJ was dead when you called me last night."

"The accident was under investigation."

"It's splashed all over the papers, television and internet. You could have told me last night. Instead I have to see it on TV."

"Well, you know now." Buford didn't have the time for the rock star's tantrum.

"They killed her. JJ was too good a driver. You'd better check the brakes on that car. I already warned them that I was going to tell you."

Buford loved nothing better than being told what he

needed to do. But he was reminded of the lack of skid marks on the highway. It had appeared that the driver of the car hadn't braked.

"Who are *they?*" he asked, even though he suspected he knew.

"Her former band members. The more I've thought of it, the more I think one of them killed Martin and then sabotaged JJ's car and killed her, as well."

"I thought you were convinced JJ killed Martin," he reminded him.

"Well, she could have after what he did to her. But if anyone is murderous, it's the members of her former band. They hated her enough as it was. Once they found out that JJ wasn't doing any reunion tour—"

"They knew that for sure?"

"I don't know. But if Martin told them and they figured out that he'd used them—"

"Mr. Atkins—"

"Check the brakes on her car. I'm telling you one of them or all three of them killed her. You should have seen their faces this morning at breakfast when I asked them which one of them did JJ in."

Buford groaned. "Please let me do the investigating."

"Let me know what you find out about the brake line."

"YOU MUST BE STARVED," LOGAN said after he and Blythe returned from their horseback ride. They'd eaten elk steak sandwiches late the night before, but that had been hours ago now. "I'll make us something to eat."

"Can I help?" She had picked up the newspapers he'd brought home earlier.

"No, you've had a strenuous enough day. Anyway, it's a one-man kitchen. I'm thinking bacon, scrambled eggs and toast." He liked breakfast any time of the day, especially at night.

"Yum." She sounded distracted.

He left her sorting through the newspapers on the couch and went into the kitchen. The sun had long set, the prairie silver in the twilight. Blythe must be exhausted. He hadn't meant to take her on such a long ride. But she'd been a trooper, really seeming to enjoy being on horseback.

It wasn't until the meal was almost ready that he realized he hadn't heard a peep out of her. She must have fallen asleep on the couch.

He put everything into the oven to keep it warm and was about to go check on her when he smelled smoke. Hurriedly, he stuck his head into the living room to find her feeding the fire she'd started in the fireplace.

"I hope you don't mind," she said quickly, no doubt seeing his surprise. "I felt a little cool."

"Sure," he said, but noticed she'd used one of the recent newspapers he hadn't had a chance to read instead of the old ones stacked up next to the kindling box by the fireplace. Also she'd made a pitiful fire. "Here, let me help you."

She'd wadded up the front pages of the most recent *Great Falls Tribune* and set the paper on fire, then thrown a large log on top. The paper was burning so quickly there was no way it would ignite the log.

He pulled the log off. The newspaper had burned to black ash.

"Oh, I'm sorry. You probably wanted to read that," she said behind him.

"Probably wasn't any good news anyway," he said not wanting to make her feel bad.

"Don't bother to make a fire," she said. "I'm fine now. What is that wonderful smell coming from the kitchen?"

He studied her a moment. "You're sure?"

She nodded.

He told himself it was his imagination that she looked pale. Earlier she'd gotten some sun from their long ride and her cheeks had been pink. Now all the color seemed to have been bleached out of her. She seemed upset.

"Maybe I'll teach you how to build a fire while you're here, too."

Her smile wasn't her usual one. "That's probably a good idea."

As they went into the kitchen, he couldn't shake the feeling that her purpose in burning the newspaper had nothing to do with a chill. It seemed more likely that it had been something she'd read in the paper.

Logan tried to remember the headlines he'd scanned before riding back to the house. Scientists were predicting a possible drought after low snowfall levels. A late-season avalanche had killed a snowmobiler up by Cooke City. Some singer named JJ had been killed in a car wreck in the Flathead Valley.

He couldn't imagine why any of those stories might

have upset her and told himself he was just imagining things. Who got upset about an article and burned the newspaper?

"Are you sure I can't help?"

He started at the sound of her voice directly behind him and checked his suspicious expression before he turned. "Nope, everything is ready." When he studied her face, he was relieved that her color had come back. She looked more like that laid-back, adventurous woman who'd climbed onto his motorcycle yesterday.

"I hope you're hungry," he said as he handed her a plateful of food.

But something had definitely ruined her appetite.

"Blythe," Logan said after they'd eaten and gotten up to put their dishes in the sink. He touched her arm, turning her to face him. She was inches from him. She met his gaze and held it. "Tell me what's going on with you." He saw her consider it.

But then her expression changed and even before she closed the distance between them, he knew what she was up to. Her lips brushed over his cheek, the look in her eyes challenging. She put her palm flat against his chest as she leaned in again, lips parted and started to kiss him on the mouth.

He grasped her shoulders and held her away from him. "What was *that?*" he demanded.

"I just thought…"

"If you don't want to tell me what's really going on with you, fine. If you want to make love with me, I'm all for it. But let's be clear. When you come to my bed, I want it to be because you want me. No other reason."

Disbelief flickered across her expression. He knew he was a damned fool not to take what she was offering—no matter her reasons. The woman was beautiful and just the thought of taking her to bed made his blood run hotter than a wildfire through his veins.

He wanted her. What man wouldn't? But he wouldn't let her use sex to keep him at a distance. Even as he thought it, he couldn't believe it himself. Why did he have to feel this way about this woman?

Her eyes burned with tears. "I appreciate everything you—"

"Don't," he said. "I'm glad you're here. Let's leave it at that. I'm going to check the horses."

BLYTHE COULDN'T ESCAPE upstairs fast enough. Just his touch set something off in her, while the kindness in his eyes made her want to confess everything. She had wanted to bare her soul to him.

Instead, she'd fallen back on what she'd always done when anyone got too close. She had tried to use the same weapon her mother had: sex. To her shock and surprise, Logan wasn't having any of it. He'd shoved her away and what she'd seen in his gaze was anything but desire. Anger burned in all that blue. Anger and disappointment. The disappointment was like an arrow through her heart.

He'd gone out to check the horses and she'd hurried upstairs to run a bath before she did something crazy like confess all. How would he feel about having a murderess under his roof? Worse, a coward? She'd gotten at least one person killed, maybe two, if she counted Martin.

Even the hot lilac-scented water of the clawfoot tub couldn't calm her. She was still shaken and upset about the almost kiss. Logan had seen right through her. Another man, she thought, would have taken what she was offering and not cared what was going on with her. But not Logan.

He saw through her. No doubt he'd also figured out why she'd burned the newspaper. She couldn't believe what she'd read in the paper. A young woman had apparently stolen her rental car, lost control and crashed, the poor woman, and now everyone thought it had been her and that she was dead?

Not her. *JJ*. The fantasy performer that Martin Sanderson had created. Now they were both dead.

She'd seen the way Logan had looked at her when she'd attempted to destroy the news articles in the fireplace. But she couldn't let him see either story—not the one about JJ's sports car convertible ending up down a rocky embankment, catching fire and killing its driver or about Martin Sanderson's murder.

When the bath water cooled to the point where she was shivering, she got out and, wearing Logan's robe, went to his bedroom. On the way, she listened for any sound of him on the couch below. Nothing. Maybe he was still out with the horses.

Still embarrassed, she was glad she didn't have to face him again tonight. Once in his bedroom, she moved to the window of the two-story farmhouse and looked out at the night. She still felt numb. What had she thought would happen when she left everything in the car beside the lake?

Nothing. She hadn't thought. If she had, she would have realized that someone could have come along, found the car, the keys, her purse and thought she'd killed herself in the lake. Instead, someone had taken the car and died in it.

How could she have ever suspected something like that was going to happen? Still she felt to blame. Someone else was dead because of her.

She remembered what it had said in the article. The police had speculated that the woman had been driving too fast and had missed the curve. Officers were investigating whether drugs and alcohol might have been involved.

Not her fault.

She sighed, close to tears, knowing better. Just like Martin Sanderson being dead wasn't her fault. Now she wished she'd been able to keep the newspaper article, to read it again more closely, but she'd panicked. If Logan saw it he might connect the car she'd been driving with this woman's death—and her. She wasn't ready to tell him everything. If she ever was.

Maybe the best thing she could do was clear out. He didn't need her problems, and eventually those problems were going to find her here. She didn't kid herself. All burning the articles had done was buy her a little time. Logan was too smart. He was going to figure it out. Eventually the police would figure it out, as well.

Isn't it possible Fate is giving you a second chance?

JJ was dead and she was alive.

She had wanted out of her life and she'd been given a chance to start over. A clean slate. With everyone thinking she was dead, she could start life fresh. Did it matter that she didn't deserve it?

As she turned away from the bedroom window, she recalled her conversation with Martin. "I would give anything to do it differently."

He'd laughed. "You're what? Barely thirty and you're talking as if your life is over? Save the drama for when you get paid for it. I'm not letting you out of your contract. Period. If you keep fighting me, I'll make you do a reunion tour with your former Tough as Nails band."

She'd been shocked he would even threaten such a thing. "You wouldn't do that."

"Wouldn't I?"

"You can't make me," she'd said, knowing that Martin Sanderson could destroy her and he knew it.

"I'll sue you, and take every penny I made for you."

"Take it. I'm done," she'd said and meant it.

He'd studied her for a moment. "Okay, you're not happy. I get it. So let's do this. Take some time tonight to unwind. Go into town. Have some fun. Then sleep on it. If you feel the same way in the morning, then… well, we'll work something out that we can both live with."

She remembered her relief. She'd actually thought things might be all right after all. Isn't that why she'd gone to that country-western bar that night? And luck had been with her. She'd met Logan Chisholm.

But by the next morning everything had changed. Martin was dead and she'd realized that she had worse problems than getting out of her contract and a tour with her former band members.

She didn't know what she would have done if Logan hadn't shown up when he did at the Grizzly Club. It had been desperation and something just as strong— survival—that had made her abandon her car and get on the back of his motorcycle. She had wanted to run away with him. Just ride off into the sunset with the cowboy from her girlhood dreams.

Now another swift change of luck. Everyone thought JJ was dead.

Especially her former band members.

Even if they suspected she was still alive, they wouldn't think to look for her in this remote part of Montana.

A bubble of laughter rose in her chest as hot tears burned her eyes. She was too exhausted to even think, let alone decide what to do tonight. She would decide what to do tomorrow. She moved to the bed. She was a survivor. Somehow she would survive this, as well. Or die trying.

As she climbed between the sheets, she didn't fight the exhaustion that pulled her under. The last thing she wanted to think about was what a mess she'd made of that old life. Or the look on Logan's face when she'd tried to kiss him.

SHERIFF BUFORD OLSON WAS IN his office when he got the call from the coroner's office.

"I've just spoken with the state crime investigators. Martin Sanderson's death has been ruled a suicide," the coroner said without preamble. "He was dying. Cancer. His personal physician confirmed my findings. He'd known he had only a few weeks to live."

Buford ran a hand over his thinning hair. All the evidence had been there indicating a suicide—except for the note. Because someone had taken it.

The moment he'd seen the safety pin with the tiny piece of yellow sticky note stuck to it, he'd thought suicide. But again, without the note…

Martin Sanderson had been shot in the heart—and not through the robe. For some unknown reason suicide victims rarely shot themselves through clothing.

The gun found at the scene was registered to Sanderson. Its close proximity to the body, the lack of evidence of a struggle, the powder burns around the wound, the gun powder residue on the victim's hands and the sleeves of his robe all pointed toward suicide.

Even the angle of the shot appeared to be slightly upward, like most suicides. Another sign of a possible suicide was the single shot to the heart. All the scene had needed was a reason for the suicide, and now the coroner had provided it. Sanderson was dying. If only they had that damned note, this case could have been tied up a lot sooner.

"Good work," the mayor said when Buford gave him the news. "Case closed. I'll alert the media."

Closed as far as the mayor was concerned, Buford thought after he hung up. But there was that missing note and the mystery of who—and why—the person had taken it. If it had been Sanderson's guest Jennifer "JJ" James, then they would never know what the note said.

Buford told himself it didn't matter. Martin Sanderson's death had been ruled a suicide. The infamous JJ had died in a car wreck. All the loose ends had been neatly tied up. What more did he want?

With a curse, he called the garage where Jennifer James's car had been taken and asked the head mechanic to check to see if someone might have tampered with the brake line.

Chapter Seven

The next day Logan was still angry with himself and Blythe. Why wouldn't she let him help her? Stubborn pride? He, of all people, understood that.

What bothered him was that the night he'd danced with her, he'd seen a strength in her that had drawn him. Now though she seemed scared. What had happened between their last dance and now? Something, and whatever it was had her on the run and hiding out here with him.

He couldn't help but feel protective of her. Whatever she needed, he would do his best to give it to her if she would just let him. He was worried about her. But he told himself the woman he'd danced with was too strong and determined to let whatever had happened beat her. Maybe she just needed time.

As for what had happened last night… He'd wanted to kiss her, wanted her in his arms, in his bed. He was still mentally kicking himself for pushing her away. He could imagine what his brothers would have said if they'd heard that he turned down a beautiful, desirable woman.

But Blythe wasn't just any woman.

And he'd meant what he'd said last night. He wanted more than just sex with her. Logan chuckled, thinking again about what his brothers would say to that.

Speaking of his brothers, he thought with a curse. One of the Chisholm Cattle Company pickups was coming down the lane in a cloud of dust. As the truck drew closer, he recognized his brother Zane behind the wheel.

He glanced toward the stairs. Blythe hadn't come down yet this morning. He'd hated the way he'd left things last night. But by the time he'd come in after mentally kicking himself all over the ranch yard, her door upstairs had been closed, the light off.

Late last night, unable to sleep, he'd decided that whatever Blythe was running from had something to do with an article in yesterday's newspaper. He'd ridden down this morning, but today's paper hadn't come yet. Maybe the best thing to do was go into town to the library so he could go through a few days papers on the internet. He couldn't imagine what she was hiding, just that she was here hiding because of it.

Now, though, he had a bigger problem, he thought as he stepped out onto the porch and walked down the steps to cut his brother off at the pass.

"Hey, what's going on?" Zane asked as he climbed out of the pickup. "Dad said you called and needed a few more days off."

"Is there a problem?"

"We're shorthanded, that's the problem," his brother said as he glanced toward the house. "Dad wants one of us staying around the main house to keep an eye on

Emma until some agency in Billings can find someone to come up here and live in the guest wing."

"He's still worried about Emma?" Their lives had been turned upside down the past six months, but should have calmed down after Aggie Wells had drowned in the creek. Once winter runoff was over, they'd find her remains and then that would be the end of it.

Logan knew his stepmother had been put through hell and all because of his father's past. But then again, she should have asked a few more questions before she'd run off with him for a quickie marriage in Vegas.

He thought about Blythe and realized he'd put himself in the same position Emma had. What did he know about the woman now sleeping in his bed? And had he let that stop him?

"You know Dad," Zane said.

"Can't today. Sorry."

"Oh?" His brother looked past him. "Emma was worried you were sick. She wanted to send some chicken soup along with me. I got out of there before she baked you a cake, too."

"I'm fine."

Zane looked at him suspiciously. "How was the Flathead?"

"Pretty this time of year."

His brother laughed. "I see you bought yourself some new clothes."

Logan looked to where Zane was pointing and swore under his breath. Blythe had left her jean jacket with the embroidered flowers on it lying over the porch railing.

His brother was grinning from ear to ear. "I knew you wanting time off had something to do with a woman."

Just then, as luck would have it, Blythe came out the front door onto the porch.

Zane let out a low whistle. "It's all becoming clear now," he said under his breath. "Aren't you going to introduce me?" When Logan said nothing, his brother stepped around him and called up to the porch, "Hello. I'm Logan's brother Zane, but I'm sure he's told you all about me."

Blythe smiled. "As a matter of fact, I think he said you were his favorite."

Zane laughed. "I like her," he said to Logan. "Why don't you bring her to supper tonight. I'll tell Emma to set another plate."

Logan could have throttled him. Zane knew damned well that if he'd been ready to tell her about the family, he would have already brought her by the house.

"Oh, and I'll cover for you today, but I'll expect you back to work tomorrow. You get babysitting duty." With that Zane climbed into his pickup, waved at Blythe and drove away.

SHERIFF BUFORD OLSON WAS about to leave his office for the day when he got another call from the coroner's office. What now, he thought as he picked up.

"The woman's body found in that car accident wasn't Jennifer James," the coroner said in his usual all-business tone. "This woman was in her early twenties. The crime lab took DNA from a hairbrush Jennifer

James left at the Grizzly Club. This Jane Doe is definitely not the woman the media calls JJ."

"We have no idea who she is?"

"She was wearing a silver bracelet with the name Susie on it. I would suggest sending her DNA to NDIS to see if they have a match. That's the best I can do." The National DNA Index System processed DNA records of persons convicted of crimes, analyzed samples recovered from crime scenes as well as from unidentified human remains and analyzed samples for missing person cases.

"Thanks," Buford said, still processing this turn of events. If JJ hadn't died in her rental car, then where was she? She'd have to be on the moon not to hear about the accident that had allegedly claimed her life at the edge of Flathead Lake. So why hadn't she come forward?

He'd barely hung up when he got a call from a gas station attendant in Moses Lake, Washington.

"Is this the sheriff in that town where JJ was killed?" a young female voice asked.

"Yes?" he said, curious since the dispatcher had motioned to him that he might actually *want* to take this call.

"Well, I wasn't sure if I should call or not, but I just had this guy in an old pickup buy gas? The thing is, he used one of JJ's credit cards. It has her on the front, you know one of those photos of her with her guitar, the kind you can get on certain credit cards? I have all her CDs, so I recognized her right off. The man tried to use the card at the pump but it didn't work so he brought it in and when it was denied again, he just took off."

Buford felt his heart racing, but he kept his voice calm. "Did you happen to get the plate number on the pickup?"

"Yeah. He didn't look like the kind of guy JJ would have dated, you know?"

"Yeah." He wrote down the license plate number she gave him and thanked her for being an upstanding citizen. She gave him a detailed description of the pickup driver. He told her to hold on to the credit card and that he'd have someone collect it from her shortly.

Even before he ran the plates on the pickup, he suspected it would be stolen—just like the credit card. It was.

Buford put an all points bulletin out on the pickup and driver, then sat back in his chair and scratched his head. JJ wasn't dead. At least her body hadn't been found, and right now Logan Chisholm might be the only person who could tell him where she went that day after leaving the Grizzly Club.

When he called directory assistance and no listing was found, he put in a call to the Chisholm Cattle Company.

LOGAN DIDN'T WANT HER meeting his family, Blythe thought with no small amount of surprise. She'd been so busy hiding her former life and who she'd been from him, she'd never considered that he might be hiding her from his family and friends.

"You can get out of it," she said as Zane drove away.

"Out of what?" Logan asked, clearly playing dumb.

She smiled. "Out of taking me to supper with your family."

"It isn't what you think." He dragged his hat off and raked his fingers through his thick blond hair. He wore his hair longer than most cowboys, she thought, but then again she didn't know many cowboys, did she? His eyes were the same blue as the sky. She'd met her share of handsome men, but none as appealing as this one.

"You don't have to explain. We just met. We don't even know each other. There is no reason I should meet your folks." Even as she said it, she was curious about his family. Curious about Logan. She felt as if she'd only skimmed the surface, but she liked him and wouldn't have minded getting to know him better—if things were different.

The thought surprised her. She hadn't had roots since she left home at fourteen and thought she didn't want or need them. But being here with Logan had spurred something in her she hadn't known was there.

"Is there any coffee?" she asked as she turned back toward the house.

"Blythe, it isn't that I don't want you to meet them."

In the kitchen, she opened a cupboard and took down a cup. She wasn't kidding about needing some coffee. She felt off balance, all her emotions out of kilter. She could feel him behind her, close.

She turned to him. "Look, you don't really know me. Or I you. I don't even know what I'm doing staying here. I should go." She started to step past him, but he closed his hand over her arm and pulled her close.

His alluring male scent filled her, making her ache with a need to touch him and be touched. She turned to find him inches from her. He took the coffee cup from her hand and set it on the counter. Then he pulled her to him.

He felt warm, his shirt scented with sunshine and horse leather. His hands were strong as they cupped her waist and drew her close. As his mouth dropped to hers, she caught her breath. She'd known, somewhere deep inside her, that when he kissed her it would be like rockets going off. She hadn't been wrong.

Logan deepened the kiss, his arms coming around her. He stole her breath, made her heart drum in her chest, sending shivers of desire ricocheting through her. She melted into his arms. He felt so solid she didn't want him to let her go.

As the kiss ended, he pulled back to look into her eyes. "I've wanted to do that since the first time I saw you."

Her pulse was still thundering just under her skin. She wanted him and she knew it wouldn't take much for him to swing her up into his arms and carry her upstairs to that double bed of his. Just the truth.

She took a step back, letting her arms slip from around his neck. She almost didn't trust what she might say. "I'm sorry about last night."

He shook his head. "I just want us to be clear. I want you. I have from the moment I laid eyes on you at the country-western bar."

"I want you, too. And I want to tell you everything. I just need some time to sort things out for myself."

He grinned and shoved back his Stetson. "And I want to take you home to meet my family, but I need to warn you about them."

"No, don't spoil it. Let me be surprised," she joked.

"I called my stepmother. We're on for tonight. But you might change your mind about everything once you meet them all."

She knew it was crazy, but she was relieved he wanted her to meet his family. It was dangerous. What if one of them recognized her? Blythe knew she had worse worries than that.

And yet, right now, all she wanted to think about was meeting Logan's family. "I need to go into town and get myself something to wear." She hadn't been this excited about a date in a long time.

Logan seemed to hesitate, as if he was thinking about kissing her again. Desire shone in his eyes. Her own heart was still hammering from the kiss. She *did* want him. More than he could know. But he wanted more from her than a roll in the hay. When was the last time she'd met a man like that?

"I better go start the truck," he said.

She was glad now that she'd stuffed a few hundred dollar bills into the pocket of her jeans before she'd left Martin Sanderson's house that awful morning. It seemed like weeks ago instead of days.

Blythe took a sip of the coffee, needing the caffeine to steady her after the kiss. She hadn't slept well last night, and the sound of the vehicle coming down the road this morning had made her heart race until she reminded herself that not a soul in the world knew she was here—other than Logan.

Now his brother Zane knew, and soon so would his family. But they knew her as Blythe. She heard the pickup door slam, the engine turning over, and downed the rest of the coffee. She felt nervous about meeting Logan's family and unconsciously touched a finger to her lips.

She couldn't help smiling as she thought of his kiss.

You're falling for this cowboy.

No, she told herself, as messed up as her life was, she couldn't let that happen. Once he knew the truth about her, that would be the end of it. Maybe she should go to the door and call him back in and tell him everything. Nip this in the bud before it went any further and they both got hurt. Tell him before she met his family.

Logan would be hurt enough once he knew everything. How long did she really think she could keep that old life a secret, anyway? What if someone in town recognized her?

Blythe put down her cup and pushed out through the screen door to the porch to pick up her jean jacket from where she'd left it. As she did, she looked out at this wide-open land. It was like her life now. Wide open. Now that she had this new life—at least for a while— she was surprised by what she wanted to do with it.

She had put away most of the money she'd made in an account where she could get to it. She could do anything she pleased, go anywhere in the world. To her surprise, though, she realized she didn't want to leave here, didn't want to leave Logan. She wanted to meet his family.

Couldn't she just enjoy this life for a little while?

As she headed out to the pickup, she saw him sitting behind the wheel. He smiled at her and her heart took off in a gallop as she climbed into the cab next to him. She knew this couldn't last, but was it so wrong for just another day?

LOGAN HAD SOME TIME TO KILL while he waited for Blythe to shop for clothes. He'd offered to buy her anything she needed, but she'd told him she had money.

"Nothing fancy," he'd warned her. "You're in the real Montana now."

After he'd left her, he'd headed to the library. He felt a little guilty, but he had to know what had been in the newspaper Blythe had burned. She was in trouble. He felt it at heart level. The only way he could help her was to know what had her running scared. Something in that newspaper had upset her. He was sure of it.

It didn't take him long at the library to find the section of the paper Blythe had burned. He scanned the articles. One caught his eye—the one about the woman who'd been killed in a car wreck at the edge of Flathead Lake. Was it possible Blythe had known the woman? He read the name. Jennifer James. Apparently she was best known as JJ, a rock star who shot to meteoric fame.

According to the story, she'd missed a curve and crashed down a rocky embankment, rolling multiple times before the car burst into flames and finally came to rest at the edge of the lake. The infamous JJ was believed to have been driving at a high rate of speed. It was not determined yet if she was under the influence of drugs or alcohol.

All it said about this JJ person was that she had led a glittering life in the glare of the media after her skyrocketing career. She had died at the age of thirty.

It wasn't until he focused on the sports car convertible that he knew he'd been right about something in the newspaper upsetting her.

The sight of the car stopped him cold. That and a sentence in the cutline under the photograph. JJ had been discovered by legendary music producer Martin Sanderson. Sanderson was a resident of the Grizzly Club, an exclusive conclave south of Bigfork.

That's when Logan saw the second headline: Famous Music Producer Found Dead.

He quickly scanned the story until he found what he was looking for. Martin Sanderson had been found dead in his home Saturday.

Saturday? The day Logan had gone to the club looking for the mysterious woman from the bar. The day Blythe had come tearing out of the gate to race down the highway like a crazy woman, then climb on the back of his motorcycle and ask him to take her away with him.

He hurriedly read the article. Investigators from the Missoula Crime Lab had been called in on the case. They thought it was a homicide? He checked to see the estimated time of death. Saturday morning.

Logan groaned. No wonder she'd wanted to get as

far away from the Flathead as possible. She'd known the sheriff would be looking for her.

The article mentioned that Sanderson had discovered the recently deceased JJ who, according to sources, had been visiting Sanderson at the Grizzly Club.

His heart began to pound as he reread the first newspaper article. Who had died in the car? Someone named Jennifer James better known as JJ, according to the story. He double-checked the car photo. It was the same make and color as the one Blythe had left beside the highway two days ago. No way was that a coincidence. Add to that the connection to the Grizzly Club...

Logan shook his head. Blythe had to have known this woman. But then why not say something? Because she felt guilty for leaving the car for her friend? They both must have been staying at the Grizzly Club with Sanderson.

So who was this JJ? From the grainy black-and-white photo accompanying the short article, it was impossible to tell much about her, since she was duded out in heavy, wild makeup and holding a garish electric guitar.

Logan glanced at his watch. He'd told Blythe he would pick her up back on the main drag after running a few errands of his own. He still had thirty minutes, enough time to see what else he could learn about the woman who had been killed.

He typed in Pop Singer JJ. Pages of items began to come up on the computer screen. He clicked on one and a color photograph appeared.

His breath rushed out of him as he stared at the photograph in shock. Blythe. No wonder he hadn't recognized her. He wouldn't have ever connected the woman who'd climbed on the back of his motorcycle with this one even without the wild makeup and masks she wore when she performed.

He thought about her that first night at the Western bar in her new cowboy boots. There had been a look of contentment on her face as she'd danced to the music. No, she'd looked nothing like this woman in the publicity photo.

It didn't help that he wasn't into her kind of music. He'd never heard of JJ or a lot of other singers and bands she'd performed with, since he was a country-western man himself.

But who was this woman staying with him really? The infamous JJ? Or the woman he'd come to know as Blythe? He had a feeling that whoever she was, she was still wearing a mask.

At least now he knew why she'd run. It had to have something to do with music producer Martin Sanderson's death. Had she killed him?

He didn't want to believe he'd been harboring a murderer. But with a curse, he reminded himself that everyone thought she was dead and she had let them. She'd seen the article. She knew someone else had died in her car. If she was innocent, then why hadn't she said something? Why hadn't she come forward and told the world she was still alive?

AGGIE WELLS WOKE COUGHING. Sun slanted in the crack between the curtains. She'd fallen asleep in her chair again and lost another day. But what had brought her out of her deathlike sleep was that same horrible nightmare she'd been having for weeks now.

She sat up, fighting to catch her breath.

The doctor had said that the pneumonia had weakened her lungs. The gunshot wound had weakened her body. Add to that failure and she felt like an old woman, one foot in the grave.

"You have to call Emma," she said when she finally caught her breath.

Call and tell her what? That you had a horrible dream—most of it unintelligible, but that you've seen how it all ends?

Aggie realized how crazy that sounded. She had nothing new to tell Emma or the sheriff. No one believed that Laura Chisholm was alive, let alone what she was capable of doing.

The nightmare seemed to lurk in the dark shadows of the room. Aggie pulled her blanket around her, but couldn't shake the chill the dream had left in her bones.

She remembered glimpses of the nightmare, something moving soundlessly in a dark room, the glint of a knife. Aggie shuddered. She hadn't seen Laura in the shadows, but she'd sensed something almost inhuman.

Aggie reached for the phone, but stopped herself. She was sure the sheriff would be tracing any calls coming into the ranch. Hoyt might answer. She might not even get a chance to talk to Emma at all.

And what would be the point? She didn't know where Laura Chisholm had gone or who she had become. She just knew the killer was headed for Chisholm ranch soon and Emma would never see her coming.

All calling would accomplish was to give the sheriff Aggie's own location. She couldn't bear the thought of spending what was left of her life in the state mental hospital or behind bars in prison.

In her weakened state, she didn't have the energy to escape again. Nor could she go out and find Laura Chisholm again for them. Just the thought of Laura Chisholm made the hair stand up on the back of her neck. She shifted in her chair. She realized sitting there that somehow she'd gone from being the hunter to the hunted.

It wasn't what Laura was capable of that terrified her. It was that the woman could somehow be invisible— until it was too late for her prey. It took a special talent to go unnoticed. To seem so safe that she didn't even stir the air, didn't appear to take up space, didn't seem to exist in any form other than a ghost.

Maybe the worst part was that Aggie *knew* Laura. She'd become Laura when she'd believed Hoyt Chisholm had killed his first wife. Aggie had worn the woman's same brand of perfume and clothing, had her hair cut in the same style, had learned everything she could about Laura. She'd tried on the woman's skin.

She *knew* Laura and, she thought with a shudder, Laura knew *her.*

A lot of people thought Aggie Wells was dead.

Laura Chisholm wasn't one of them.

In Aggie's nightmare, Laura found her.

Chapter Eight

Logan's cell phone rang, echoing through the small, quiet library. He quickly dug it out, saw that it was his stepmother calling and hurried outside to take it. "Hello."

"Where are you?" Emma said sounding excited about having company tonight.

"In town. Blythe—" She might be the pop rocker JJ, but he thought of her as Blythe and knew he always would. "Had to get something to wear for tonight."

"You didn't tell her she had to dress up, did you?" Emma scolded.

"Just the opposite. But she's a woman. You know how they are."

His stepmother laughed. "We're looking forward to meeting her."

Logan wanted to warn Emma not to get too attached to her—just as he'd been warning himself since she'd climbed on his motorcycle. Since finding out who she really was, he was even more aware that she would be leaving soon, possibly prison. If innocent, back to her old life. No woman gave up that life to stay in his old farmhouse—no matter what she said.

"So you're still in town," Emma said.

"I have to pick up Blythe at the clothing store in about fifteen minutes and then we were headed back to my place."

"Don't do that. Come on over to the main house so we can visit before supper," she said. "Anything you want to tell me about this woman before you get here?"

He chuckled. "Nothing that comes to mind."

"Oh, you," Emma said. "Zane says she's lovely."

"She is that." And mysterious and complex and let's not forget a star—and quite possibly a murderer. Right now a star who is being immortalized because she died so young.

"Is this serious? Your brother seems to think—"

"Zane really should stop thinking," he snapped, realizing that Blythe wouldn't just be lying to him tonight at supper at the main ranch. She would be lying to his family. Involving them in this mess.

"I didn't mean to pry," Emma said, sounding a little hurt.

"You did, but that's what I love about you," he said softening his words. Emma was the best thing that had happened to their family. She only wanted good things for all of them.

"I just remembered an errand I have to run," Logan said, and got off the phone.

He checked his watch and then hurried back in the library. He wanted to check today's paper and see if there was anything more about Martin Sanderson's and JJ's deaths.

Logan found the most recent edition of the *Great*

Falls Tribune. Both JJ and Martin Sanderson had made the front page.

Mayor Confirms Music Producer's Death a Suicide

A tidal wave of relief washed over him as he quickly read the short update. Blythe might be JJ, but at least JJ wasn't a murderer. He knew that should make him happier than it did. There was a long article about JJ, about her humble beginnings, her rise to stardom, her latest attempts to get out of her contract and how she had died too young.

Her fans had been gathering across the country, making memorials for her. Logan remembered the waitress at the Cut Bank café and swore. The woman had recognized her. That's why Blythe had made them hightail it out of there.

But if she hadn't killed Martin Sanderson, then what was she running from? Was her life that bad that she'd rather let even her fans believe she was dead rather than come forward? Better to let them think she had died in a fiery car crash?

He realized that the whole world believed that the infamous JJ was dead. Everyone but him, Logan thought with a groan.

The only thing to do was call the sheriff over in the Flathead and let him know that JJ was alive. He started to reach for his cell phone and stopped himself. He couldn't do anything until he confronted her.

As he left the library, he recalled what she'd said to him when they'd reached Whitehorse that first night.

"Have you ever just needed to step out of your life for a while and take a chance?"

Is that what she was doing? Just taking a break from that life? Good thing he hadn't gotten serious about her, he told himself as he drove down the main drag and saw her waiting for him on the sidewalk ahead.

As he pulled in, she turned in a circle so he could see her new clothes. She was wearing a new pair of jeans, a Western blouse and a huge smile.

It was easy to see why he would never have recognized her even if he had followed pop rock. She looked nothing like the JJ of music stardom. Her dark hair was pulled back in a ponytail, her face, free of makeup, slightly flushed, her faded-denim blue eyes sparkling with excitement.

He felt a heartstring give way at just the sight of her.

"What do you think?" she asked as she slid into the cab next to him. "I don't want to embarrass you at supper. Is it too much?"

"You look beautiful."

She beamed as if that was the first time anyone had ever told her that.

"Emma called." Logan was going to tell her that supper was canceled but she instantly looked so disappointed, he couldn't do it. He had let her pretend to be someone she wasn't this long, what were a few more hours? "She wants us to come on by."

"If it's okay with you, sure," she said brightening. "Can you believe it? I'm nervous about meeting your family."

She wasn't the only one who was apprehensive, Logan thought as he drove out of town. At least he wasn't taking an alleged murderer to meet his family.

But he didn't have the faintest idea who this woman really was or what she was doing in Whitehorse. Once supper was over and they were back at the house—

"I have great news," she announced as he started the motor. "I have a job. I saw a Help Wanted sign in the window just down the street, I walked in and I got the job."

He stared at her. The sign down the street was in the window of a local café. "You took a *waitress* job?" He'd expected that she would tire of being the dead star soon enough and come out of hiding. He'd never expected this.

"I've slung hash before," she said sounding defensive. "It's been a while, but I suspect it's a little like riding a bike."

He didn't know what to say. Did she really hate her old life that much? Or was she still hiding for another reason?

"Tomorrow, if you'll give me a ride to town, I'll find myself an apartment so I can walk to work. As much as I've loved staying with you…"

Logan had driven out of Whitehorse, the pickup now rolling along through open prairie and sunshine. He hit the brakes and pulled down a small dirt road that ended at the Milk River. Tall cottonwoods loomed over them, the sunlight fingering its way through the still bare branches.

As he brought the truck to a dust-boiling stop, he said, "You can drop the front. I know who you are, JJ. So what the hell is really going on?"

SHERIFF BUFORD OLSON couldn't believe he was still sitting in his office waiting for phone calls. His stomach grumbled. He'd missed lunch and he didn't dare go down the hall to the vending machine for fear of missing one of those calls he'd been waiting for.

When his phone finally rang, he was hoping it would be Logan Chisholm. It wasn't.

"We picked up Charlie Baker," the arresting officer told him. The man who'd tried to use JJ's credit card at the gas station in Moses Lake, Washington. "He has several warrants out on him from Arizona and he's driving a stolen pickup."

"I just need to know where he got the credit card he tried to use for gas in Moses Lake," Buford said.

"He says his girlfriend took it from a purse she found in a convertible parked next to Flathead Lake. He swears the car keys were on the floorboard and that his girlfriend took the car, wrecked it and died."

"Did he say what his girlfriend's name was?"

"Susie Adams."

Now at least Buford knew who was lying in the morgue. What he didn't know was where JJ was, why she left her car beside the lake or why she hadn't turned up yet.

He thought about what Jett had said about checking the brake line on her rental car. Jett thinking that someone had tampered with the car bothered him.

First Jett was so sure JJ had killed Martin. Now he was sure that JJ had been murdered. The man just kept changing his tune. Why was that?

After Buford hung up from talking to the officer who'd picked up Charlie Baker, he called the garage and asked for the head mechanic.

"Tom, anything on that convertible yet?"

"You had it pegged," the mechanic said. "Someone tampered with the brakes."

That explained why the woman driving the car hadn't appeared to brake.

As he hung up, Buford wondered how it was that Jett had suspected foul play. Was he also right that one of JJ's former band members was behind this? Apparently they all had it in for JJ, including Jett.

The big question now was: where was JJ? And how long before whoever tried to kill her tried again?

BLYTHE TURNED TO HIM, THOSE blue eyes wide with surprise, then regret.

"We both know your name isn't Blythe."

Her chin came up. "It's Jennifer *Blythe* James."

The afternoon sun shone into the truck cab, illuminating her beautiful face. "Why didn't you just tell me you were this JJ?" he said with a curse.

Her smile was sad. "I'm sorry I kept it from you."

"Why did you?"

She shook her head. "It's such a long story."

He shut off the engine. "I have nothing but time."

Looking away, she said, "You wouldn't believe me if I told you."

"Try me."

With a sigh, she turned to face him again. "I saw a chance to put that life behind me—for even a little while. I took it."

"Who was Martin Sanderson to you?"

"He was my music producer. Basically he owned me

and my music," she said with no small amount of bitterness.

"You knew he was dead before you got on the back of my bike, didn't you?"

She nodded. "I didn't kill him, if that's what you're thinking."

"That was exactly what I thought, but his death has been ruled a suicide."

The news took her by surprise. "*Suicide?* No, that can't be right. Martin wouldn't—"

"Apparently he had cancer and only weeks to live."

She shook her head, letting it all sink in, then she smiled. "The bastard. That explains a lot. He insisted I come to Montana so we could talk about him letting me out of my contract. He was threatening to destroy my career—such as it was—and take everything I've made. I didn't care. I just wanted him to let me go."

"Did he?"

"Just before I met you that night at the bar," she said with a nod. "He told me to go have some fun and that if I didn't change my mind, then he would try to work something out with me in the morning." She let out a humorless laugh. "He knew he wouldn't be around by then."

"So you don't know how he left it."

She shook her head. "It doesn't matter. I'm done. If he sold my contract to someone else, let them take me to court. If they want, they can take every penny I made. I don't care." She smiled. "I have a job as of today. I don't need more than that."

Logan liked her attitude. He just wasn't sure he believed she could go from being rich and famous to being poor and unknown.

"Anyway, it probably doesn't matter," she added with a shake of her head.

"What do you mean, it probably doesn't matter?"

Again she looked away. He reached over to turn her to face him again. "What aren't you telling me? What was the real reason you ran away with me?"

"I told you. It was my girlhood fantasy to run away with a cowboy," she said.

He shook his head. "The truth, Blythe."

She swallowed, her throat working for a moment, then she sat up a little straighter as if steeling herself. "Someone has been trying to kill me."

BUFORD FELT HIS BELLY RUMBLE again with hunger. Clara was still putting hot chile peppers in everything, but he was building up a tolerance apparently. He couldn't wait to get home for supper, but he didn't want to leave until he heard back from Logan Chisholm.

When his phone rang, he thought for sure it would be Chisholm calling him back. He'd left a message at the ranch and been assured by Emma Chisholm that she would have her stepson call as soon as she saw him.

Instead the call was from a waitress from a café in Cut Bank, Montana.

"I saw in the newspaper that JJ was dead?"

"Yes?" Apparently she hadn't seen the latest edition.

"Well, that's weird because I saw her that day, you know, the day it said she died?"

Buford thought of the missing hours between when

she'd left her car beside the lake and when she'd left Martin Sanderson's house.

"What time was that?"

"It was late afternoon."

Cut Bank was hours from Flathead Lake. "Where was this that you saw her?"

"Here in Cut Bank at the café where I work. I recognized her right off, even though she pretended it wasn't her. I guess I scared her away. I should have been cooler."

"Scared her away? You saw her leave?"

"Yeah, I watched her and her boyfriend leave on his motorcycle."

Bull's-eye, Buford said under his breath. "What did the boyfriend look like?" He listened as she described a blond cowboy on a Harley, the same description the guard at the Grizzly Club had given him. Logan Chisholm.

"Did you see what direction they were headed?" he asked.

"East."

East, toward Whitehorse, Montana. East, toward the Chisholm Cattle Company ranch.

Buford thanked her for calling. The moment he hung up, he called Sheriff McCall Crawford in Whitehorse.

BLYTHE HAD FEARED HOW LOGAN would take the news. She had to admit he'd taken it better than she'd suspected. He was angry with her, but it was the disappointment in his expression that hurt the most.

"Someone is trying to kill you?" He sounded skeptical. She couldn't blame him. She didn't want to get into this with him, but she could see he wasn't going to take no for an answer.

"I started getting death threats a few months ago. I didn't think too much about it. People in the glare of the media often get letters from crazies." She shrugged, and she could see that he was trying to imagine the life she'd been living.

"Something happened to convince you otherwise," he said.

"There were a series of accidents on the road tour. The last time I was almost killed when some lights fell. You have to understand. I had wanted to quit for months. I guess that was just the last straw."

"You went to the police, of course."

"I did, but then Martin leaked the story to the media and it turned out looking like a publicity stunt. For a while, I thought it was. I thought Martin had hired someone to scare me back in line."

"Martin Sanderson really would have done something like that?" Logan asked, clearly unable to comprehend it.

She let out a humorless laugh. "Martin was capable of anything, trust me."

Logan took off his Stetson and raked a hand through his hair. "The note you dropped at the café in Cut Bank, is that part of this?"

She couldn't help her surprise.

"Yeah, I picked it up. It didn't seem important until now. *You're next?*"

"It was pinned to Martin's robe the morning I found

him lying dead next to the fireplace. I thought whoever had killed him—"

"Was coming after you next." Logan nodded. "That explains the way you came flying out of the club and why you climbed on the back of my motorcycle."

"Not entirely. When I saw you… I wanted to run away with you and would have even if none of this had happened." She could tell he wanted to believe that, but was having a hard time.

"You thought whoever killed him left the note for you."

She nodded.

"Why do I get the feeling that you know who's after you?"

She looked into his handsome face. It had been so long since she'd opened up to anyone. When had she become so mistrustful? She'd told herself it was the dog-eat-dog music business that had turned her this way. It was hard to know who your friends were, since it felt as if everyone wanted a piece of you.

But she trusted Logan. He hadn't asked anything of her. Still wasn't.

"I made a lot of mistakes in my life, especially when I signed with Martin Sanderson. Ten years ago, I was in a small all-girl band called Tough as Nails with some friends. Then Martin 'discovered' me." She couldn't keep the regret from her voice. "I wanted to get away from my life so bad then that I signed on the dotted line without thinking, let alone reading the contract. I dumped the band and my friends, latched onto that brass ring and didn't look back."

He frowned. "So you think this is about your former band members? Why now? Why wait ten years? Unless something changed recently."

She loved how quickly he caught on. "Martin was waiting up for me the night after I met you at the bar. He had some news, he said. He was planning to get Tough as Nails back together for a reunion tour and he'd invited them to Montana to knock out the details. He said after that, then he would let me out of my contract."

"You refused."

"I didn't trust him, let alone believe him. I'd lost track of the other members of the old band. As far as I knew, they'd all moved on, and since I hadn't heard anything about them, I'd just assumed they weren't involved in the music industry anymore." She looked out the side window for a minute. "Also we hadn't parted on the best of terms. They felt like I deserted them. I did."

"Still that doesn't seem like enough to want you dead."

She laughed. "You really don't know the music business." She quickly sobered. "But you're right. There *was* more. There was this young musician who was part of a band that we used to open for. His name was Ray Barnes. He'd been dating my best friend in the band and the others, as well. When I left, he left, too. With me. Today he's best known as Jett Atkins."

JETT ATKINS. LOGAN REMEMBERED seeing JJ with Jett in one of the photographs he'd uncovered on the library internet. "So you and Jett are—"

"History. A long time ago. But another one of my regrets."

"Who was the girl he was dating?"

"Karen Chandler, or Caro as we called her. But I think he might have been seeing the others at the same time. He was like that." Logan heard her remorse, saw the pain. He could understand why she had wanted to start her life over. "I don't want to believe it is Karen, but I hurt her badly. She and I grew up together. I should have fought harder for the band. After I left, it fell apart. Any one of them probably wants me dead."

Logan shook his head. "Isn't it possible the band would have fallen apart even if you'd stayed?"

"We'll never know, will we? But if Martin was telling the truth, then he got their hopes up. He was threatening to tell them I refused to be part of the band anymore, that I was too good for them. It wasn't true, none of it. He admitted he had never planned a reunion tour of Tough as Nails. He was just using them to get back at me."

Martin Sanderson really had been a bastard. He played with people's lives with no regard for them. Logan could understand why Blythe had wanted out, why she had felt desperate. Especially after Martin had apparently killed himself. Had he tried to make it look as if she had murdered him? Then why the note, he asked, voicing his thoughts.

"When I found Martin dead and saw the note pinned to his body…" She shuddered. "I couldn't be sure his killer wasn't still in the house and that I *was* next."

"So you think he wrote the note? Or someone else?"

She shrugged. "Maybe it was his final hateful act."

"I'm glad I was there when you needed me, but you can't keep running from this, Blythe. You have to find out who's after you—if they still are—and put an end to it. The Flathead County sheriff is going to figure out that you weren't in that car, if he hasn't already."

She nodded. "I would have told you the truth, but I wanted you to like the girl who always wanted to ride off into the sunset with a cowboy."

"I *do* like her," he said as he reached across the seat for her. "I like her a lot." He cupped her cheek, his thumb stroking across her lips.

She leaned into the warmth of his large callused hand and closed her eyes. Desire thrummed through her veins.

"Blythe?" His voice was low. The sound of it quickened her pulse.

She opened her eyes. Heat. She felt the burn of his gaze, of his touch.

He dragged her to him and dropped his mouth to hers. She came to him, pressing against him with a soft moan. Her arms wrapped around his neck as he deepened the kiss and her blood turned molten.

"I want you," she whispered when he drew back. "Here. *Now*."

Chapter Nine

"Come on," Logan said as he opened the pickup door and pulled Blythe out behind him. Warm sunlight filtered through the new leaves of the cottonwoods. A warm spring breeze whispered softly in the branches as he led her along the riverbank.

At a small grassy spot, he turned and drew her close. His face was lit by sunlight. She looked into Logan's handsome face and felt her pulse quicken.

She'd wanted this from that first night they'd danced together at the country-western bar. There was something about this man. Being in his strong arms, she'd never felt safer—and yet there was a dangerous side to him. This man could steal her heart and there was nothing she could do about it.

As he pulled her closer, she swore she could feel the beat of his heart beneath his Western shirt. Her nipples ached for his touch as they pressed against the lace of her bra. His kiss, at first tender, turned punishing as the fever rose in both of them.

She grabbed the front of his shirt and tore it open, the snaps giving way under her assault. She pressed her palms to his warm, hard chest, breathing in the very male scent of him along with the rich primal scents of the riverbottom.

Logan pulled back, his gaze locking with hers, as he tantalizingly released each of the snaps on her Western shirt. She felt her blood run hot as his gaze dropped to her breasts. He freed one breast from the bra, his mouth dropping to the aching nipple. She arched against him, moaning softly like the trees in the spring breeze.

As he slid her shirt off her shoulders, he unhooked her bra freeing her breasts, and pulled her against him. Blythe reveled in the heat, flesh against flesh, as they stripped off the rest of their clothing, then dropped down in the sweet, warm grass.

Later she would remember the wonderful scents, the soft sounds, the feel of the Montana spring afternoon on her bare skin. But those sensations had been lost for a while in the fury of their lovemaking. It was Logan's scent, his touch, his sounds that were branded in her mind forever.

LOGAN LET OUT A CURSE AS HE checked the time. They had been snuggled on the cool grass as the sun disappeared behind the Bear Paw Mountains in the distance.

They got up, brushing off their clothes and getting dressed by the edge of the river.

"This might have been a better idea after the family supper," Logan said, but he was grinning. He picked a leaf out of her hair, laughed and then leaned in to kiss her softly on the mouth.

"Keep that up and we won't make supper at all," she

said, teasing. She would have been happy to stay here by the river forever.

Once in the pickup, she snuggled against him again as he drove toward the family ranch. Logan seemed less nervous about taking her home to meet his family. That was until they turned and passed under the large Chisholm Cattle Company sign and started up the road to the house.

She felt him tense and realized that she hadn't been paying any attention as to where they were going. Looking up now, she saw a huge house come into view. She tried to hide her surprise. She couldn't help but glance over at Logan.

"Nice place," she said playing down the obvious grandeur. Was this why he didn't want her to meet the family? He didn't want her to know that they were obviously well off? The irony didn't escape her.

As the front door of the house opened, a short, plump redhead in her fifties stepped out onto the porch.

"My stepmother, Emma," Logan said as he parked and cut the engine. Opening his door, he reached for Blythe's hand and she slid out after him. He squeezed her hand as they walked toward the house as if he was nervous again. She squeezed back, hoping there wasn't any reason to be.

"This must be Blythe," Emma said, pulling her into a warm hug. "Welcome to our home."

She felt herself swept inside the warm, comfortable living room where she was introduced first to Logan's father, Hoyt. He was just as she'd pictured the rancher, a large man with blond hair that was turning gray at the temples, a sun-weathered face and a strong handshake.

The brothers came as a surprise. Blond and blue-eyed, Colton resembled Logan and Zane and their father, but the other three had dark hair and eyes and appeared to have some Native American ancestry.

"You really do have five brothers," she whispered to Logan as they were being lead into the dining room.

"We're all adopted," Logan said.

That came as a surprise too, and she realized how little they knew about each other. It was the way she'd wanted it, actually had needed it. But that was before. Now she found herself even more curious about him and his family.

With the fiancées of the brothers Tanner, Colton, Marshall and Dawson, the dining room was almost filled. She was thinking how they would have to get a larger table if this family kept growing and at the same time, she couldn't help thinking of her own family table—TV trays in front of the sagging couch.

What was it like growing up with such a large family? She felt envious of Logan and wondered if he knew how lucky he was. A thought struck her. How could he ever understand her and the life she'd led? He'd always had all this.

Dinner was a boisterous affair with lots of laughter and stories. She couldn't remember a more enjoyable evening and told Emma as much.

"I'm new to the family myself," Emma confided. "Hoyt and I were married a year ago May."

Blythe could see that the two were head-over-heels

in love with each other. On top of that, it was clear that everyone at the table adored Emma, and who wouldn't?

"This meal is amazing," Blythe said. "Thank you so much for inviting me."

Logan had been quiet during supper. She wondered if he was always that way or if he felt uncomfortable under the circumstances. He wouldn't want to lie to his family, so keeping her secret must be weighing on him.

But when their gazes met, she saw the spark she'd seen earlier by the river and felt her face heat with the memory of their lovemaking.

"So I understand that Logan has taught you to ride," Hoyt said drawing her attention.

"She was a natural," Logan said sounding proud.

"I had a wonderful instructor and I loved it," she gushed. "I love the freedom. All this wide-open country, it's exciting to see it from the back of a horse."

"Where are you from that you don't have wide-open country like this?" Emma asked.

Blythe had known someone was bound to ask where she was from. "Oh, we had wide-open country in southern California. Desert. It's not the same as rolling hills covered with tall green grass and huge cottonwoods and mountains in the distance dark with pine trees."

"What do you do for a living?" Hoyt asked. Emma shot him a look. "I don't mean to be rude," he added.

"I'll get dessert," Emma said, rising from her chair.

Blythe smiled and said, "I don't mind. I've done a lot of different things, but today I got a job in town at the Whitehorse Café. I'll be waitressing."

"Waitressing's a good profession," Emma said, and shot her husband a warning look.

Blythe excused herself and went into the kitchen to help Emma get the dessert. The rest of the meal passed quickly and quite pleasantly.

It wasn't long until she was saying how nice it was to meet everyone, how wonderful the meal was and promising to come back.

"Oh, Logan, it slipped my mind earlier," Emma said as she pressed a bag full of leftovers and some freshly baked gingersnaps into his arms as they were leaving. "You had a call earlier from a Sheriff Buford Olson from Flathead County. He needs you to call him. I put the number on a slip of paper in the bag with the food. He said it was important."

LOGAN HAD SEEN BLYTHE'S panicked expression when Emma mentioned the call from the sheriff in Flathead County. He drove out of the ranch and turned onto the county road wondering why the sheriff was calling him, and realized the guard at the Grizzly Club had probably taken down the plate number on his motorcycle.

He glanced over at her, saw she was looking out at the night and chewing at her lower lip. "The sheriff knows. Or at least suspects I know where you are."

Blythe nodded. "I'll call him."

What if she was right and someone really was trying to kill her? She was safe here.

"It's too late now. Let's call him in the morning," he said.

They made love again the moment they reached the

house, both of them racing up the stairs to fall into his double bed.

Lying staring up at the cracked ceiling, Logan smiled to himself. His body was damp with sweat and still tingling from her touch.

Blythe was lying beside him. She sighed, then let out a chuckle.

Logan glanced over at her and grinned. "What's so funny?"

"Us," she said. "We both lied about who we are. You were afraid I was after your money. I was afraid you would only be interested in JJ."

"Pretty funny, huh," he said.

She nodded.

He studied her for a moment, then pulled her over to spoon against her backside. His breath tickled her ear, but she giggled, then snuggled closer.

"I love the feel of you. I can't remember a time I've felt happier."

Logan felt the same way. He breathed in her warm scent, languishing in her warmth and the feel of her flesh against his, and tried not to worry.

But if she was right and someone wanted her dead, then as soon as everyone knew she was alive, Blythe wouldn't be safe. He couldn't bear the thought of any harm coming to her.

She would be safe here with him.

That was if she didn't go back to her old life.

The thought was like an arrow through his heart.

Of course she would go back.

He felt his heart break. He'd fallen for this woman from the moment he'd seen her on that dance floor only days ago.

"WE CAN'T KEEP LIVING LIKE THIS," Emma Chisholm said after everyone had left. She'd said this before, but this time she saw that Hoyt knew she meant it.

"The house is armed to the teeth with weapons," she continued. "You never leave my side or have one or two of my stepsons here watching me."

She wasn't telling him anything he didn't already know, but she couldn't seem to stop. "You have done everything but build a dungeon and lock me in it. I can't leave here without an armed guard. You're killing me, Hoyt, and worse, I see what it is doing to you."

He nodded as if he knew she not only meant it, but that he could see the strain this had put on their family.

"I know you're sick to death of me hanging around," he said.

"It's not you. It's knowing that you should be working this ranch and not babysitting me. Your sons are going crazy, as well. They need to be on the back of a horse in wild country, not cooped up here in this kitchen. And I need to do something besides bake!"

He smiled then as if he'd noticed the extra weight she was carrying. "I like your curves."

"Hoyt—"

"I have some news," he said quickly. "I was going to tell you tonight. I found a woman through that service in Great Falls. She sounds perfect, older, with experience cooking for a large family. The service explained how isolated we are out here and that it would be a live-in position and she was fine with that."

Emma didn't necessarily like the idea of someone living in the house with them. But the house was large. The woman would have her own wing and entrance and they would all have plenty of privacy. Anyway, what choice did Emma have?

She knew Hoyt flat out refused to leave her alone. It was nonnegotiable, as he'd said many times. If this was the only way she could have some freedom, she would take it. It was at least a step in the right direction.

"Wonderful. I could use the help," she said agreeably.

Hoyt eyed her suspiciously. "She comes highly recommended. She will be doing the housework and helping with the cooking, if you let her. She'll accompany you wherever you need to go."

Emma mugged a face, but was smart enough not to argue.

He smiled and moved to embrace her. "I'm so sorry about all of this."

"Stop that. None of this is your fault."

His expression said he would never believe that. "If Laura is alive, if she's what Aggie believed she was, then it has to be my fault. I failed her. Failed all of us, especially you."

Emma was surprised to hear him even entertain the idea that his first wife might be alive. He'd sworn he didn't believe it. Apparently she wasn't the only one living with ghosts.

She shook her head and took her husband's face in

her hands. "Listen to me. We can't know what's in another person's heart let alone their mind, even those closest to us. You said yourself that Laura was like a bottomless well when it came to her need. No human can fill that kind of hole in another person."

He leaned down to kiss her.

"So when do I meet my new guard?" she asked.

"She's coming at the end of the week."

Emma hated the idea, but at least Hoyt and his sons could get back to running the ranch. She would deal with the housekeeper and find a way to get some time away from the ranch—alone.

She couldn't live her life being afraid, thinking every person she met wanted to kill her. Emma had lost some of her old self and she intended to get it back.

Not that she was going to take the gun out of her purse that was always within reach. She was no fool.

AGGIE WELLS HAD BEEN DOZING in her chair. She jumped now at the sudden tap on her door. Holding her breath, she waited. Another light tap.

Aggie realized it was probably her doctor friend coming back to check on her. He'd wanted to put her in the hospital but she'd refused, knowing that would alert the authorities and be the end of her freedom.

With effort, she pushed herself up out of the chair and moved to the window. Parting the curtain, she peered out, surprised that it was dark outside.

Even in the dim light, she could see that it wasn't the doctor. It was the elderly woman who lived in the unit at the end of the building. The old woman was horribly stooped, could barely get around even with the gnarled cane she used. She wore a shawl around her shoulders, a faded scarf covering most of her gray hair.

Aggie had seen her hobbling by, headed for the small store a few blocks away. She'd thought about helping the woman but everyone who lived in the old motel units kept to themselves, which was fine with her.

The old woman tapped again, so bent with age and arthritis that she probably saw more of her shoes than she did where she was going. For a moment she leaned into the door as if barely able to stand, then tapped again, swaying a little on her cane, and Aggie realized she must need help or she wouldn't be out there.

Aggie quickly opened the door. "Is something wrong?" she inquired, reaching for the elderly woman's arm, afraid the woman was about to drop onto the concrete step.

But the moment she grabbed the arm she realized it wasn't frail and thin but wiry and strong.

Aggie had always been a stickler for details. Too late she noticed that while everything else was like the old woman's who lived a few doors down, the shoes were all wrong.

Chapter Ten

The woman Aggie Wells had opened the door to brought the cane up, caught her in the stomach and drove her back into the room. She quickly followed her in, closing and locking the door behind them.

As the formerly stooped woman rose to her full height, she shrugged off the shawl and faded scarf. Aggie saw why she'd been fooled. The shawl and faded scarf were *exactly* like the old woman's who lived in the last unit.

She let out a cry of regret, knowing that the old woman wouldn't be in need of either again.

Aggie had stumbled when she'd been pushed and fallen, landing on the edge of the recliner. Weak and gasping for breath, she now let herself slide into the seat while she stared at the old woman's transformation into a woman nearer her own age. It was a marvel the way Laura Chisholm shed the old woman's character.

"We finally meet," she said to Laura, realizing the woman must have known where she was for some time. Laura had been watching and waiting for just such an opportunity.

Only the shoes would have given her away, had

Aggie noticed them before she opened the door. Laura Chisholm's feet were too large for the old woman's shoes. When she'd disposed of the poor old woman, taken the shawl and scarf and cane, she'd had to use her own shoes.

There was a time when Aggie wouldn't have been fooled. She would have noticed the small differences and would never have opened the door. But that time had passed, and a part of her was thankful that she had finally gotten to meet a woman she'd unknowingly been chasing for years.

"Aggie Wells," Laura said, as if just as delighted to meet her.

How strange this feeling of mutual respect, two professionals admiring the other's work.

"Just tell me this," Aggie said, not kidding herself how this would end. "Why?"

"Why?" Laura cocked her head almost in amusement. There was intelligence in her blue eyes but also a brightness that burned too hot.

"Do you hate Hoyt that much?"

Laura looked surprised. "I *love* Hoyt. I will *always* love him. Haven't you ever loved someone too much and realized they could never love you as much?"

Aggie hadn't. Other than her job. "Let me guess, everything was fine until he adopted the boys."

Laura's face darkened. "I wasn't enough. First it was just three boys, then three more. He said he had enough love for all of us." She scoffed at that.

"You could have just divorced him and made a life for yourself."

Laura smiled. "Who says I haven't?"

"But you couldn't let go. You've been killing his wives." There was no accusation in her voice. She was just stating what they both knew.

Laura looked down at the thick gnarled wood cane in her hand, then up at Aggie. "If I couldn't have him, no one else could either."

"Why didn't you just kill him?"

The woman looked shocked at the idea. "I *loved* him. I couldn't do that to him."

But killing his wives was another matter apparently. "I'm curious. How did you get away that day at the lake?"

Laura frowned and waved a hand through the air as if the question was beneath Aggie. "I told Hoyt I was afraid of water, that I couldn't swim. He believed anything I told him. I grew up in California on the beach and learned to scuba dive in college. I set everything up beforehand, the scuba gear, the vehicle on a road a few miles from the spot where I would go overboard. I simply started an argument with Hoyt and let the rest play out. When he realized that I'd filed for divorce, it made him look guilty. I thought he would never remarry. I was wrong."

She shrugged, and Aggie realized what Laura had been able to do since then was much more impressive. Laura had dedicated her life to making sure Hoyt found no happiness with another woman.

Just as Aggie had dedicated hers to chasing the truth. Other people had balance in their lives, they had their job, their family, their friends, but not her and Laura.

They'd both sacrificed their lives for something intangible: a cockeyed sense of being the only ones who could get justice.

Was this woman's quest any crazier than her own? Aggie had lost the job she loved because she couldn't let go of that thin thread of suspicion that something wasn't quite right about Laura Chisholm's death.

Had she been able to let go, where would she be now? Certainly she wouldn't be wanted for murder, nearly committed to a state mental hospital and about to die at the hands of the real killer.

And Laura? Had she felt loved, wouldn't she still be with Hoyt, raising six sons, getting old with him in that huge house on the ranch?

"We don't choose this, it chooses us," Aggie said seeing the truth of it.

Laura nodded as if she had been thinking the same thing.

Then again Laura might simply be crazy.

The difference now was that Laura would win.

"Has it been worth it?" That was the real question Aggie had wanted to ask. She watched Laura lift the thick wooden cane and step toward her.

"Worth it?" Laura asked as she closed the distance between them. A smile curled her lips, her eyes now bright as neon. "What do you think?"

Aggie's last thought was Emma. She said a quick prayer for her. The fourth wife of Hoyt Chisholm didn't stand a chance against a woman this obsessed.

LOGAN WOKE TO FIND HIS BED empty. For just an instant, he thought he'd dreamed last night. But Blythe's side of the bed was still warm, her scent still on his sheets. He heard the soft lap of water in the tub of the adjacent bathroom, then the sound of the water draining, and relaxed.

A few moments later Blythe came out, her wonderful body wrapped in one of his towels. He grinned at her and pulled back the covers to pat the bed beside him.

"Sorry, but I have to call the Flathead sheriff, then get to work, and so do you," she said, reaching for her clothes. "Zane said you have Emma duty today."

He couldn't believe she was really going to go to that waitress job, but he was smart enough not to say so. With a groan, he recalled that she was right. He had Emma duty today. He much preferred working on the ranch than hanging out at the house. Today though, he much preferred staying in bed with Blythe. He reached for her, thinking they had time for a quickie.

She giggled, pretending to put up a fight.

At the sound of a vehicle coming up the road, they both froze. "Are you expecting anyone this morning?" she whispered.

He shook his head and reluctantly rose from the warm bed to pull on his jeans. Going to the window, he looked out and felt a start. It was a sheriff's department patrol SUV coming up the road. He watched it grow closer until he could see the sheriff behind the wheel. She had someone with her.

He swore under his breath as he hurriedly finished dressing.

"Who is it?" Blythe asked sounding worried.

"The sheriff. She has someone with her. I'll go see what they want."

"You know what they want."

He gave her a smile he hoped was reassuring, kissed her quickly and went downstairs. He'd wanted to call the sheriff before anyone found out that JJ was staying with him. He figured it would look better for Blythe.

As the patrol car came to a stop in front of his house, he stepped out onto the porch. "Sheriff," he said as McCall Crawford climbed out. He felt as if he'd seen too much of her during the mess with his father's former wives.

"Logan."

His gaze went to the big older man working his way out of the passenger seat. He was big-bellied, pushing sixty, his face weathered from years in Montana's sun.

The man merely glanced in Logan's direction before reaching back into the patrol car for his Stetson. As he settled it on his thinning gray head, he slammed the patrol car door and stepped toward the house.

"This is Sheriff Buford Olson from the Flathead County," McCall said. "We're here about Jennifer James. JJ?"

Logan nodded as the door opened behind him and Blythe stepped out.

JETT ATKINS GROANED AT THE sound of someone knocking on his motel room door. It was that damned sheriff, he thought as he went to the door. Sheriff Buford Olson acted as if he wasn't all that sharp. But Jett wasn't fooled.

He hurriedly hid the suitcase he'd had by the door. The sheriff hadn't told him he could leave town yet—even after Martin Sanderson's death had been ruled a suicide. It was that damned JJ. The sheriff had said he was waiting for the coroner's report.

All Jett knew was that he'd had enough of this motel room, this town, this state. He wanted to put as much distance as he could from whatever Martin had been up to with JJ's former band members.

But when he opened the door, it wasn't the sheriff. Loretta stood in the doorway.

"What are you—"

She didn't give him a chance to finish as she pushed past him. He closed the door and turned to find her glaring at him. It reminded him of all those years ago when the two of them had dated. Well, he wouldn't really call it dating. More like what people now called hooking up.

"Where's JJ?" she demanded.

"What are you talking about? She's dead."

"You haven't seen the news today?"

He hadn't. He was sick of sitting in this room with nothing to do but watch television. Last night he'd packed, determined to leave town no matter what. Then he'd finished off a half quart of Scotch and awakened with a hangover this morning. He hadn't even turned on the TV.

"No, why?" he asked now. Loretta said she sang in a bar and nightclubs. He knew she was just getting by. He'd shuddered at the thought, since it was his greatest fear. At least she hadn't been famous and had the rug pulled out from under her. Most people hadn't even heard of her or Tough As Nails.

"That body that was found in JJ's rental car turned out to belong to some woman from Arizona. The cops think the woman stole JJ's car and crashed it. I heard just now that they are investigating the crash as a homicide."

He had to sit down. He lowered himself to the edge of the bed. "You're saying someone tried to kill JJ but killed some other woman instead? Then where is JJ?"

"That's what I just asked you."

"I haven't seen her. She was gone by the time I reached Martin and found him dead…" He stared at Loretta. "I wasn't joking about one of you wanting her dead."

Loretta rolled her eyes. "If I wanted to kill her, it would be more personal than a car wreck. I'd want to be the last person she saw before she died."

He shuddered. "Maybe you were."

She scoffed at that. "I vote for Betsy. That sweet act of hers? I've never bought it. It's women like that who kill, you know."

He didn't know. He figured any of the three were capable of it. Especially if they acted together.

"Or Karen," Loretta said, as if she'd been giving it some thought. "After all, JJ was her best friend—or so she thought. Also, I heard that Martin went to Karen first." She nodded at his surprise. "Karen had the talent. But I heard she turned him down flat, saying she could never desert JJ."

Jett let out a low whistle. "Then JJ deserted her without a thought."

Loretta shrugged. "There is another possibility," she said eyeing him intently. "You."

He laughed. "Why would I want to kill JJ?"

"According to the tabloids, she dumped you."

"Do you really believe *anything* you read in them?" he challenged. "Anyway, that was just the spin Martin put on it after *I* dumped JJ." He could see Loretta was skeptical. "You have no idea what it's like to date someone with her kind of star power. It was exhausting."

"She did outshine you, didn't she?" Loretta said with no small amount of satisfaction.

"Well, whoever tried to kill JJ…apparently they failed," Jett said. "And now she's disappeared."

"So it would appear," Loretta said mysteriously.

"If you know where she is, then why were you asking me?" he demanded.

She smiled. "I just wanted to see if you knew where she was. You don't. She'll turn up. She owes me for this mess and I intend to get my money out of her, one way or another." With that she left, slamming the door behind her.

"WE WERE GOING TO CALL YOU this morning," Logan said as Sheriff Buford Olson's gaze went to Blythe.

"Is that right?" he said, not sounding as if he believed it for an instant. "I think we'd better sit down and talk about this."

"Do you mind if we come in?" McCall asked.

Logan shook his head. "Come on in. I'll get some coffee going."

"So why don't we start with you telling me who you are," Buford said after they'd all taken chairs and cups of coffee at the kitchen table.

Blythe braced herself as she looked into the sheriff's keen eyes. "My name is Jennifer Blythe James, but I think you already know that."

"JJ," he said. "Okay, now tell me what you're doing here."

"Getting on with my life," she said.

"You do realize that you left the scene of a death without calling anyone, then left the scene of an accident that resulted in another death, not to mention let everyone believe you were dead."

"At first I panicked," she admitted. She had felt no need to clear her name. Not her name, JJ's. How strange. JJ had become a separate persona over the past ten years. Blythe had lost herself and only found that girl she'd been the other night at a country-western bar dancing with Logan Chisholm.

But she doubted the Flathead sheriff would understand that.

"I'd been getting death threats and having some close calls on my music tour," she continued. "I was convinced someone was trying to kill me. Martin had made it appear that the incidents were nothing more than a publicity stunt. I left the tour and came to Montana to try to talk him into letting me out of my contract. I'd had enough."

Sheriff McCall Crawford sipped her coffee and

didn't say a word. Clearly, she'd just come to bring the Flathead sheriff.

"Did you talk him out of it?" Buford asked.

Blythe shook her head. "I thought I had. But that night when I returned to the house, he told me he had contacted the members of my former band and was going to make me do a reunion tour with them if I didn't go back on my music tour. I told him to stuff it and left the room."

"Did you hear the shot that killed him?"

"No, that house is too large, I didn't hear a thing. I didn't know he was dead until I came back down to the living room the next morning and saw him."

"Saw him and the note pinned to him," Buford said. "What did the note say?"

She had to quell a shudder at the memory. *"You're next."*

The sheriff studied her. "Why did you take the note?"

"I don't know. I grabbed it before I thought about what I was doing, wadded it up and stuck it in my pocket. I guess it made everything a little less real. Then I realized that whoever had killed him could still be in the house. So I ran. I thought if I could get far enough away from there, go some place that no one knew about…"

"That was pretty shortsighted," Buford said.

She nodded and glanced at Logan. "I just wanted to escape my life for a while. By the way, Logan didn't know anything about what I was running from or even who I was."

"Did you recognize the handwriting on the note?" Buford asked.

A chill snaked up her spine. Hadn't she known how vindictive Martin was? How deceitful? The man had made his fortune using other people and their talents.

"No," she said. "I just assumed the person who'd killed him was the same one who'd been threatening me. Now I think he might have written the note himself."

"Why would he do that?" Buford asked.

"He wanted me to fear for my life. I think he killed himself hoping I would be under suspicion for his death." If it hadn't been for fate and a car thief, she might have been arrested.

"You're that sure he wrote the note," the sheriff said. "What about his other guests?"

"Other guests?" she echoed.

"You weren't aware your former band members were staying in the guesthouse just out back?"

She could feel the color drain from her face. Reaching for her coffee, she took a drink, burning her tongue.

"So you didn't know that Karen, Loretta and Betsy had already arrived?" he said.

She shook her head.

"Is it possible one of them found the body and wrote the note?" he asked.

Blythe couldn't speak. She looked from her coffee cup to him and knew he saw the answer in her eyes.

"You said there had been death threats before this? Do you have copies of those?" he asked.

"No, I threw them away. They didn't seem...serious at the time."

"A death threat that didn't seem serious?" Buford asked.

"I've had them before and nothing happened. Other musicians I've known have gotten them. They aren't like, 'I'm going to kill you.' They're more vague, like, 'You have no idea what you're doing to the kids listening to your horrible music. Someone should shut you up for good.' That sort of thing."

"I have a granddaughter who listens to your music," Buford said. "She listens to Jett Atkins, as well. I think whoever wrote that note might have a point."

"That's another reason I wanted out of my contract," she said. "Martin had total control of my career as well as the music. I hated what I was singing. I signed the contract with him when I was very young and stupid."

"Your former band members aren't the only ones in Montana. Your boyfriend Jett is here, as well," Buford said.

"He's not my boyfriend."

The sheriff nodded. "No love lost there either, huh?"

"If you're asking if I have enemies—"

"I know you do," Buford said, cutting her off. "The brakes on your rental car had been tampered with. The death of the woman driving it has been ruled a homicide."

Blythe felt all the air rush out of her. She shot to her feet and stumbled out of the room.

"If you know someone is trying to kill her," she heard Logan say as she pushed open the screen door and stepped out onto the porch. Blythe didn't catch the rest. Logan couldn't blame the sheriff. She was the one who'd run. If she'd called the sheriff the moment she'd found Martin's body—

She heard the screen door open behind her. The next moment, Logan's arms came around her.

"Don't worry," he said as he drew her close. "I'm not going to let anyone hurt you."

"YOU CAN'T ARREST HER GIVEN the circumstances," Logan said when he and Blythe returned to the kitchen and the two sheriffs sitting there.

Buford studied him for a moment, then turned his attention to Blythe. "You should know that at least one member of your old band is dead. Lisa Thomas."

"Luca?" Blythe said.

"Apparently she died recently," Buford said. "In a hit-and-run accident."

Logan saw Blythe's expression. She had to be thinking the same thing he was. It had been no accident.

"I'm going to talk to the former members of your band again," Buford was saying, "but in the meantime…"

Blythe glanced at her watch. "In the meantime, I have a job in town I need to get to."

The sheriff raised two bushy eyebrows, but it was McCall who spoke before Logan could.

"Are you sure that's a good idea?" the Whitehorse sheriff asked. "You seem to have a target on your back."

"It's a terrible idea," Logan interrupted, but he saw the stubborn set of Blythe's jaw.

"What am I supposed to do, sit around and wait for someone to come after me again?" she demanded.

Buford chuckled as he rose slowly from the kitchen chair. "What kind of job did you say this was?"

"Waitressing." She raised her chin defiantly.

"Making it easy for whoever wants you dead to find you, huh?" He nodded smiling.

Logan stared at her. "You're using yourself as *bait?* Have you lost your mind?"

"Could I speak with you outside?" she asked.

"You betcha," he said taking her arm and leading her back out to the porch. "What the hell, Blythe?"

"I don't expect you to understand this," she said. "But ten years ago I signed away all control of my life when I took Martin Sanderson's offer to make me a star. I have that control back and it feels really good."

"You're right, I don't understand. There is someone out there who wants you *dead.*"

She nodded. "And I might have kept running like I did when I left my car beside the lake and climbed on the back of your motorcycle. But you changed that. I don't want to run anymore."

"You don't have to run. You can stay here. I will—"

Blythe leaned into him and brushed a kiss across his lips silencing him. "I need a ride to town. I hate being late my first day of work. Is that offer to lend me a pickup still open?"

He didn't know what to say. It was clear that she'd made up her mind and there was no changing it. He swallowed the lump in his throat, trying to fight back his fear as the two sheriffs came out onto the porch. All he could do was reach into the pocket of his jeans and hand her his truck key.

"I'll get one of my brothers to come pick me up," he said his voice tight.

"You sort it out?" Buford asked as Blythe headed for his pickup.

"Find out who is after her," Logan said between gritted teeth. "Find them before they find her." Meanwhile he was going to do everything in his power to keep her safe.

The problem was that the woman was as stubborn as a damned mule. But he was glad that Blythe seemed her former strong, determined self again. Not that he wasn't worried about what she would do next.

Chapter Eleven

Betsy came out of the shower to find Loretta and Karen sitting on the ends of the bed, glued to the television screen. Her heart kicked up a beat. "What's happened now?" she asked with a sinking feeling.

Loretta grabbed the remote to turn up the volume. A publicity shot of JJ flashed on the screen, then a news commentator was saying that an inside source had confirmed that the body found in the rented sports car convertible was not pop rocker JJ.

"Authorities are asking anyone with information regarding JJ to call the sheriff's department." A number flashed on the screen.

"I don't understand," Betsy said. She knew now why she never watched the news. It depressed her.

"JJ," Loretta said. "She's not dead. She wasn't driving the car that crashed."

"Then who was?" Betsy asked.

Loretta shrugged.

"Then where is JJ?" Betsy asked.

Karen looked over at Loretta. "That's the million-dollar question, isn't it?"

Loretta was already heading for the door. "I need

a drink. Call me if you hear anything. I already asked Jett about JJ. He swears he doesn't know where she is. But I wouldn't be surprised if the two of them cooked this up. When I find JJ, she is going to pony up some money for this wasted trip. I swear, that bitch is going down."

As she went out the door, Karen sighed.

"Does she really believe that Jett and JJ cooked up letting some poor young girl die in JJ's car?" Betsy asked. "Is that really what she thinks?"

"Loretta has always had her own way of thinking," Karen said distractedly. "Just as she sees this as JJ owing her."

"What do *you* think about all this?"

Karen seemed surprised that Betsy would ask her. But Karen had always seemed the most sensible one in the band and Betsy said as much.

"Thanks for the vote of confidence, but I have no idea. The police will sort it out. In the meantime, I wish I knew where JJ was."

"You miss her, don't you?"

Karen smiled. "Hard to believe after what she did to all of us, huh."

"She was just offered an opportunity and took it," Betsy said. "I don't blame her. But you were just as good as she was, if not better. I've never understood why Martin chose her and not you."

"I guess he saw something in JJ that I lacked."

"Do you still play and sing?"

"I don't really have the time," Karen said, but Betsy knew it was more than that.

"It hurt us all when the band broke up. Don't you think we could have found another lead singer? I mean, we didn't have to break up the band when JJ left."

Karen smiled as she turned back to her. "We'll never know."

"Loretta says that JJ's leaving was like having the heart ripped out of us because we felt betrayed," Betsy persisted. "Is that how you felt?"

When the door opened and Loretta came in with Jett, Betsy noticed that Karen seemed glad for the interruption. Clearly, she hadn't wanted to talk about JJ anymore. Or how she felt about the girl she considered her sister walking out on her.

"It's all over Twitter," Jett announced. "JJ was seen east of here."

BLYTHE HAD SOME TIME TO think on the way into town. She needed an apartment so she could walk to work. She couldn't keep driving around town in a Chisholm Cattle Company pickup. But she knew that wasn't the real reason she couldn't stay with Logan any longer.

She couldn't put him in any more danger than she already had.

What she'd told Logan had been heartfelt. He had changed everything. She would have kept running, but he made her want to end this so she could get on with her life—and she hoped Logan would be in it.

But until she found out who was after her, she had to put some distance between them. Whoever had put the note on Martin Sanderson's body could have killed her that morning at the Grizzly Club. She figured the only reason they hadn't was that they wanted her running scared still.

She wouldn't let them use Logan Chisholm to do it.

As she drove into the small western town of Whitehorse, she spotted the local newspaper office. The idea had been brewing all the way into town, but as she pushed open the door to the *Milk River Courier,* she was aware that what she was about to do could be the signing of her death warrant.

"Can I help you?" The young woman who rose from behind the desk had a southern accent and a nice smile.

"Are you a reporter?" Blythe asked.

"Andi Jackson, at your service," she said, motioning to the chair across from her desk.

Blythe saw that the small newspaper office was deserted as she took a seat. "You're a weekly paper? Is it possible to get a story in this week's paper?"

"It would be pushing my deadline, but if it's a story that has to run, I can probably get it in tomorrow's paper," Andi said.

"It is. My name is Jennifer Blythe James, better known as JJ, and until recently everyone thought I was dead."

Andi picked up her notebook and pen and began to write as Blythe told her JJ's story, starting with the small trailer in the middle of the desert, then a band called Tough as Nails and ending with her waitressing at the local café in town.

"This is one heck of a story," Andi said when Blythe had finished. "I'm curious how it's going to end."

Blythe laughed. "So am I." After Andi took her

photo, she bought a paper so that she could look for an apartment after work, then she headed for the Whitehorse Café. The last thing she wanted was to be late for work her first day.

"YOU AREN'T GOING TO HAVE to babysit me much longer," Emma said when Logan came through the back door into the kitchen. "Your father has hired someone to keep an eye on me so you can all get back to ranching. The woman is supposed to be here by the weekend."

She glanced at him as he dropped into a chair at the table. "Logan?"

He blinked and looked over at her as if seeing her for the first time that morning. "Sorry, I was lost in thought."

"I can see that." She'd never seen him this distracted and would bet it had something to do with the young woman he'd brought to supper last night.

Having just taken a batch of cranberry muffins from the oven, she put one on a plate for each of them and poured them both a mug of coffee before joining him at the table.

"Okay, let's hear it," she said as she sliced one muffin in half and lathered it with butter.

"It's Blythe," he said with a curse.

She laughed. "Big surprise." Emma took a bite of the muffin. It was warm and wonderful, the rich butter dripping off onto the plate as she took another bite. She really had to quit baking—worse, eating what she baked. "So you've fallen for her."

"No, that is…" He started to swear again but checked himself. "I've never met anyone like her."

"So what's the problem?"

"Someone is trying to kill her."

Emma leaned back in surprise. "It must be something in the water around here," she said, and then turned serious. "Why would anyone want to hurt that beautiful young woman?"

"It's a long story," Logan said with a sigh.

Emma listened, seeing how much this woman had come to mean to him. Chisholm men were born protectors. What they didn't realize sometimes was that they were also attracted to strong women who liked to believe they could protect themselves. Hoyt was still learning that.

"It doesn't sound like there is much you can do if she's set on doing things her way," Emma said. "But you certainly don't have to hang around here babysitting me today. I'll be just fine."

Logan shook his head, grinning across the table at her. "Blythe reminds me a lot of you."

"That's a good thing, right?" she asked with a laugh.

"Stubborn and a woman hard to get a rope on," he joked.

"You Chisholm men. When are you going to learn that you have to let a woman run free if you ever hope to hold on to her?"

"It's a hard lesson," Logan said. "I'm not sure I can do that."

"But then again, you've never been in love before.

Love changes everything. Have you told her how you feel?"

"About her determination to stick her neck out and get herself killed?"

"No, Logan, how you feel about *her*."

"It's too soon."

"Or is it because you're afraid you'll scare her off?" she asked, eyeing him.

He chuckled. "You see through me like a window-pane. You have any more of those muffins? Also, I need to borrow your computer. I have to find out everything I can about who's after Blythe. So far, they don't know where she is. But once they find out…"

AFTER HER INTERVIEW WITH THE newspaper, Blythe hurried to the café to get to work. Within minutes after putting on her apron, she was waiting tables and joking with locals as she refilled coffee cups and slid huge platefuls of food in front of them.

It *was* like riding a bike, she thought.

As she worked, she tried not to glance out the front window at the street or the small city park across from the café. The newspaper article wouldn't come out until tomorrow. Reporter Andi Jackson had told her the Associated Press would pick up the story and it would quickly make every newspaper in the state.

"You realize your story is going to go viral after that," Andi had said. "With communications like they are, everyone in the world will know that JJ is waitressing in Whitehorse, Montana."

That was the plan, Blythe thought.

Still, she couldn't help but feel a little nervous about the repercussions that were to come when Logan found out—not to mention the fact that the story was bound to bring a killer to town.

Right before quitting time, she saw Logan pull up out front. Just the sight of him as he stepped from one of the Chisholm ranch pickups made her heart take off at a gallop. She ached for a future with him. They were just getting to know each other. If she let herself, she could imagine the two of them growing old together in that farmhouse of his, raising kids who Logan would teach to ride horses before they learned to walk, just as he had done.

She could see them all around that long table at the home ranch. She'd never had siblings, let alone lived close to any cousins. She'd always wished for a large family like Logan's and guessed it wouldn't be long before Hoyt and Emma had more grandchildren running around than they could count.

"Hi," she said as she stepped outside, so glad to see him it hurt.

Logan looked into her eyes and she saw the pain in all that blue as he dragged her to him and kissed her. As he drew back, he said, "How was your first day of work?" She could tell it was hard for him to even ask.

"My feet are killing me," she said with a laugh. "How was your day?"

He gave her a look that said he couldn't take any more chitchat. "We need to talk."

Blythe nodded and they walked across the street to the park and took a bench.

"You know how much I want to protect you," he began. "But I can't if you're working here in town."

"I see what your stepmother has been going through waiting for a possible murderer to come after her," she said. "Look what it is doing to your family. I don't want that. If someone wants to kill me badly enough, they will find a way no matter what."

"No, I won't—"

"Worse, if I was with you at the time, then they might kill you, as well." She shook her head. "That isn't happening. That's why I'm getting an apartment here in town, that's why I can't see you—"

"No," he said shooting to his feet and pulling her up with him. He grabbed her shoulders and looked into her eyes. "This is hard enough. If I can't see you... No."

"It's only temporary," she said touched. "I'm sorry. You had no idea what you were getting into when you met me."

"Oh, I had some idea." He let go of her but she could see this was killing him. "What now?"

"Now I find an apartment." She hesitated, knowing what Logan's reaction was going to be when she told him about the newspaper article coming out in tomorrow's paper. "Then when the article comes out tomorrow about JJ being alive and well and waitressing in Whitehorse—"

Logan swore, ripped his Stetson from his head and raked one large hand through his thick blond hair. "You know what bothers me?" He bit off each word, anger cording his neck. "You are filled with so much guilt over leaving behind your former band members that you think you *deserve* this."

She shook her head. "You're wrong. I do regret what I did, but I'm not ready to die. I want to live, really live, for the first time in a long time," she said with passion. "You know why that is? Because of you. I can't wait for the next time I get to make love with you. That's why I'm doing this. I want it over and I don't want you in the cross fire."

He dragged her to him and dropped his mouth to hers for a punishing kiss. "You aren't going to have to wait long for the next time we make love," he said when he pulled back. "Let's find you an apartment. That article doesn't come out until tomorrow, right?"

SHERIFF BUFORD OLSON HADN'T wanted to like JJ any more than he had Jett Atkins. But the young woman he'd met on her way to her waitress job had impressed him. He couldn't help but like her—and fear for her.

He'd seen the look in her eye. She was planning to use herself as bait. Not that he could blame her for wanting to flush out the killer. He wanted that as badly as she did.

"You'll keep an eye on her," he'd said to Sheriff McCall Crawford.

McCall had nodded. "You think it's one of her former band members?"

"Likely, given what we know. They had motive and opportunity. I'll see what I can find out as far as means and get back to you. The music business sounds more dangerous than law enforcement."

"The nice thing about Whitehorse is that the town is small enough that anyone new stands out like a sore thumb. I'll be waiting to hear from you."

Buford had a lot of time to think on his way back to Flathead. The moment he reached his office, he had a call waiting for him from Jett Akins.

"Is it true?" Jett asked. "Is JJ alive and living in Whitehorse?"

The sheriff shook his head at how fast news traveled. "Where did you get that information?"

"It's all over the internet."

Of course it was. "Under the circumstances, I'm not at liberty to say."

"The circumstances? You don't think I want her dead, do you?"

"It has crossed my mind," Buford said.

"It's these women JJ should be worried about. I just went down to the room where they were staying," Jett said. "They've cleared out."

"Only the Sanderson case is closed, but I can't keep all of you in town any longer."

"That's it?" Jett demanded. "If you knew these women the way I do—"

"I heard that you dated all of them at one time or another. I guess I'm just surprised you aren't the one they want dead," Buford said.

"I'll be leaving town now, *Sheriff.*" Jett slammed down the phone in his ear.

Buford hoped that was true. With the news out on the internet, Blythe was already bait—but she might not realize it.

He put in a call to the cell phone number she'd given him. It went straight to voice mail. When he called Logan Chisholm's cell, he answered on the first ring.

THE MOMENT EMMA SAW THE sheriff drive up, she knew it was bad news. She stood in the doorway, holding the screen open, afraid to step out on the porch.

Sheriff McCall Crawford climbed out of her patrol SUV. She stopped when she saw Emma watching her, slowing as if dreading what she'd come to tell her.

"Emma," the sheriff said as she mounted the stairs. Not Mrs. Chisholm at least.

"I just made iced tea," Emma said and turned back into the house for the kitchen. She heard McCall behind her. "As I recall, you like my gingersnaps," she said over her shoulder. She wanted to avoid whatever bad news the sheriff had brought as long as possible, since she had a feeling she already knew.

She set about putting a plate of cookies on the table and pouring the tea as the sheriff took a seat at the kitchen table.

"It's about Aggie, isn't it?" Emma said as she put the tea and cookies on the table and dropped into a chair across from McCall. Zane, she noticed, was out by the barn. He was her babysitter today. She told herself the news might turn out to have a silver lining. Maybe it would put an end to this house-arrest life she'd been living.

"We found Aggie," the sheriff said.

"She's dead."

Another nod. "I'm sorry."

"Did you find her in the river?" Emma asked around the lump in her throat. Aggie. She thought of the vibrant, interesting woman, obsessed, yes, but so alive, so filled with a sense of purpose.

"No, not in the river. In Billings." The words fell like stones in the quiet room.

Emma crossed herself, mumbling the Spanish she'd grown up with, the religion Maria and Alonzo had given her.

Neither of them had touched their tea or the cookies.

"I don't understand." That was all she could think to say because she feared she *did* understand.

"She'd apparently fallen ill after going in the river."

Emma raised her gaze from the table to stare at the sheriff with an accusing look she could no longer control. "Don't you mean, after being shot by one of your deputies?"

"She was a wanted criminal who was getting away, though I'm sure the bullet wound added to her deteriorated condition," McCall said without looking away. "She was living in an old motel on the south side of Billings."

Hiding, trying to get well, Emma thought. Her stomach roiled with both grief and anger. "Is that what killed her?"

Now the sheriff looked away. "She was murdered."

"Murdered? Then you know who killed her?"

As McCall finally looked at her again, there was regret in her dark eyes. "After Aggie gave you the photos of the woman she believed was Laura Chisholm, I called in the FBI. They are tracking the woman."

"Without any luck," Emma said.

"We don't know who killed Aggie. She lived in a place where some of the residents had records for violent behavior. One of them could have killed her for a few dollars in her purse. Another woman was also killed in the same building. I wish I had better news."

She scoffed. "How could the news be any worse?"

McCall shook her head as she rose to her feet. "I'm sorry."

Emma looked at the young woman. She wanted to blame her for Aggie's death, blame someone. But if anyone was to blame, it was herself. If she'd gone to McCall and told her she was meeting Aggie...

Water under the bridge now. She studied the sheriff. "When is your baby due?"

McCall's expression softened. "November."

Emma smiled. "Do you know—"

"We want to be surprised." Her smile was strained, guarded and Emma remembered thinking McCall was pregnant once before, months ago.

"Miscarriage?" Emma said. "I'm sorry. I will keep you and your baby in my prayers."

"Thank you," McCall said, her voice thick with emotion. "I'm sorry about Aggie."

Emma nodded. She couldn't blame the sheriff anymore than she could blame Hoyt. He had called the sheriff when he suspected his wife was up to something involving Aggie that day. Emma would never forgive herself. Aggie had been trying to save her, was no doubt still trying when she was killed. The woman would never give up—that was her downfall as well as her appeal.

Apparently the person who killed her was the same way.

Emma listened to the sheriff leave, then laid her head on her arms on the kitchen table and let the hot tears come. A woman who'd tried to save her was dead and now her murderer was coming for Emma.

If Laura Chisholm had gotten to Aggie, then Emma knew there was little hope for her. Aggie wouldn't have been easily fooled. Laura would find a way to get to her and Emma doubted she would see her coming.

THE NEWS GOT OUT FASTER THAN Blythe had anticipated. Logan had told her it was all over the internet after Sheriff Buford Olson had called to warn him.

"Don't go to work today," Logan had pleaded with her. "Come out to my place. We'll take a long horse-back ride up into the mountains."

"Don't tempt me," she'd said.

"Blythe—"

"I have to go back. I'm working a split shift. Maybe I'll see you after work." There was nothing she would have liked better than staying in bed with him. Her heart ached at the thought of giving up a horseback ride with him. Yesterday they'd found her a furnished apartment and made love late into the night.

But Blythe knew the only way she could be free to be with Logan was to end this, one way or another.

Now, at work at the café, there'd been a steady stream of diners since the newspaper article had come out that morning. Most just wanted coffee and pie and to check out this pop rock star who was now waitressing in their town.

Things had finally slowed down when Blythe saw a car pull up out front of the cafe. The car caught her attention because there were so few in this Western town. Pretty much everyone drove trucks.

She'd just served a tableful of ranchers who'd joked with her and still had her smiling, when she saw the woman climb out of the car. A cold chill ran through her. Karen "Caro" Chandler.

Her former best friend from childhood was tall and slim. She wore a cap-sleeved top in a light green with a flowered print skirt and sandals. As she removed a pair of large dark sunglasses, Blythe saw that she was even more beautiful than she'd been when they were girls.

"I'm going to take my break now, if that's all right," she called over her shoulder to the other waitress. Removing her apron, she tossed it on a vacant booth seat and stepped outside.

Karen looked up as Blythe came out the door, her expression softening into a smile. "It's been a long time."

"Too long," Blythe said, and motioned to the park bench across the main street. The sun felt warm and reassuring as they crossed the street. Only a few clouds bobbed along in a clear, blue sky. The air smelling of spring and new things seemed at odds with the conversation Blythe knew they were about to have. The past lay heavy and dark between them.

"So how is waitressing again?" Karen asked. "Remember that greasy spoon where you and I worked in high school? You broke more dishes and glasses than I did. But Huck always forgave you."

"Huck," she said smiling at the memory. "I wonder whatever happened to him?"

"He died a few years ago after rolling his car on the edge of town." Karen nodded at her surprise. "I went back to the desert to take care of Dad. He had cancer."

"I'm sorry." She studied her friend, surprised not that Karen had gone back to take care of her father but that she was stronger than Blythe had ever imagined. When they were girls, Blythe had been the one who made all the decisions about what the two of them did and Karen had let her. She watched Karen brush back a lock of hair and look up toward the warm blue of the sky.

"I know why you're here," Blythe said.

"Do you?" Her former friend looked over at her, their gazes locking.

"I'm sorry. I should never have left the band, left you behind."

Karen laughed. "Is that why you think I'm here?" She shook her head, smiling. "Tough as Nails breaking up was the best thing that ever happened to me. I went to college, met a wonderful man. We live together back east. We have a good life. I'm happy, Blythe. I didn't come here to tell you that you ruined my life. Quite the opposite. After you left, I realized I could do anything I set my mind to, I didn't need you to tell me what to do anymore."

"I'm still sorry. I wish I had kept in touch," she said,

hearing bitterness in Karen's voice no matter how much she denied it. "If not to tell me how much you hate me, then why are you here?"

"Luca came to see me before she died," Karen said. "She told me something that I thought you should know. She wrote some songs when she was dating Jett. When they broke up, he took the songs."

That didn't surprise Blythe. "He must not have recorded them or—"

"He did. Right after the two of you signed with Martin. Luca went to Martin. They settled out of court. A couple of the songs were his biggest hits."

"I had no idea," Blythe said, shaking her head.

"Luca felt that she'd been swindled by Martin and Jett. She was going to go public if they didn't pony up more money. The next thing I heard, she'd stepped in front of a bus."

Blythe felt her blood run cold. "You think it wasn't an accident? That someone pushed her?"

Karen nodded. "You were with Jett during the time when he recorded the songs. Do you remember seeing Luca's small blue notebook?"

The chill that ran through her made her shudder. She hugged herself against it, the warm spring sun doing nothing to relieve the icy cold that had settled in her.

"I was afraid that might be the case," Karen said. "Luca had found out that Jett planned to release another of her songs. That is why she was so upset with Martin and Jett. Jett had told her he no longer had the notebook."

He'd lied. No big surprise there. "You think either he or Martin killed her to shut her up."

"If I'm right, then you might be the only one who saw him with that notebook of Luca's songs," Karen said. "Luca's song that he recorded is set to come out next month."

Could this explain the accidents on her road tour? Jett was always around since he'd been closing for her. And he was in Montana. But if anyone had rigged the brakes on the sports car she'd rented, it must have been Martin. Unless Jett had come to town earlier and Martin had let him into the Grizzly Club without anyone knowing it.

She would bet there was a back way out of the club, one only the residents used.

Blythe felt sick. "Thank you for telling me."

Karen shrugged. "You were once like my sister. Whatever happened after that…" She stood. "Good luck, JJ." Her tone said she thought Blythe would need it.

Karen was studying her. "You seem…different."

"I'm not JJ anymore. As far as I'm concerned, she's dead. I'm Blythe again." She'd started going by Blythe in high school because it had sounded more mature, more like the musical star she planned to be. "JJ" had been Martin's idea.

"You do know that there never was going to be a re-union tour of Tough as Nails," Blythe said.

Karen looked amused. "I knew that. I think Betsy

and Loretta did, too. Got to wonder why they came all the way to Montana, don't you."

Blythe could see that Karen was trying to warn her. Jett might not be the only who wanted her dead.

"You going to keep waitressing when this is all over?" Karen asked, sounding skeptical.

"I might. It's honest work and I think I need that right now." She didn't say it, but the next time she picked up a guitar, she hoped it would be to sing a lullaby to one of her children. With Logan Chisholm.

"If you're ever in Whitehorse again…" She realized that Karen didn't seem to be listening. She was staring across the street.

Blythe followed her gaze and saw Logan leaning against his pickup watching the two of them.

"A friend of yours?" Karen asked, turning her gaze back to Blythe. She broke into a grin. "You finally found that cowboy you always said you were going to run away with."

Blythe knew they would never be close again, not like they'd been as kids, but she hoped they stayed in touch. Maybe time would heal the friendship. She sure hoped so. Impulsively, she hugged her former friend.

Karen seemed surprised at first, then hugged her tightly. "Be careful. I hope I get to hear about this cowboy someday."

Blythe glanced at Logan. She'd asked him to stay clear of her. "He's one stubborn cowboy," she said as they started back across the street toward Karen's car.

The truck came out from behind the space between

two main drag buildings where there'd been a fire a year ago. Sun glinted off the windshield, the roar of the engine filling the spring air as the driver headed right for the two of them.

Chapter Twelve

Buford called the airport only to find that none of the four, Jett, Karen, Loretta or Betsy had taken a flight out of town. He was in the process of calling rental-car agencies when Betsy walked into his office.

"There is something I think you should know," she said. She was nervously twisting the end of a bright-colored scarf that hung loosely around her neck.

He motioned her into a chair across from his desk. "What do I need to know?"

"It probably doesn't mean anything, isn't even important," she said haltingly.

"But you're going to tell me so I can be the judge of that, right?"

She nodded solemnly. "Ten years ago I overheard a conversation. I didn't mean to. Everyone thought I'd already left. I was always slower than the rest of them at getting out after a performance."

Buford tried to curb his impatience. "What did you hear?"

"Martin Sanderson. He was making one of the band members an offer," she said.

"JJ." He quickly corrected himself. "I'm sorry, I guess she was Blythe then."

Betsy shook her head. "It was Karen. She was apparently Martin's first choice. I heard him tell her that she had more talent than Blythe and that he could make her a star."

"Karen didn't take the offer," Buford said afraid he saw how this had gone down.

"She said she couldn't do that to her friend. Martin laughed and said, 'Well, she won't feel the same way when I make her the same offer.' Karen said he was wrong. That he didn't know Blythe the way she did."

"I would imagine Karen was upset when she heard that her friend had taken the deal and not looked back," Buford said.

Betsy shook her head. "That's just it. Karen didn't react at all. We all knew she had to be devastated, but she is so good at hiding her true feelings. If anyone hates JJ, it has to be her. She was betrayed worse than any of the rest of us. So you can see why there was no way the band could survive after all that. It was clear that Karen's heart definitely wasn't into it."

Betsy had quit worrying at the end of her scarf. She got to her feet and seemed to hesitate. "Jett said JJ's car had been tampered with and that's what killed that girl who took it."

"Your point?" he asked even though he had a good idea where this was headed.

"Karen's father was a mechanic. She loved to work with him on weekends. She knew all about cars and didn't mind getting her hands dirty. One time, when they were dating, she even fixed Jett's car for him."

LOGAN HAD BEEN WATCHING Blythe and another woman he'd never seen before visiting across the street. Was the woman one of the former members of her old band? They had seemed deep in conversation, making him anxious.

When they'd finally stood, hugging before heading across the street, he'd relaxed a little. Whoever the woman was, she apparently didn't mean Blythe any harm.

Then he'd heard the roar of the pickup engine, saw it coming out of the corner of his eye and acted instinctively. Later he would recall rushing out into the street to throw both women out of the way of the speeding truck. Now as he knelt on the ground next to Blythe, his heart pounding, all he could do was pray.

"Blythe! Blythe!" When she opened her eyes and blinked at the bright sunshine, then closed them again, the wave of relief he felt made him weak.

"Blythe," he said, part oath, part thanks for his answered prayer.

"Logan," she said, opened her eyes and smiled up at him.

"Is she all right?" he heard a voice ask behind him.

"She'd better be." There'd been a few moments when she hadn't responded. They'd felt like hours. He'd never been so scared.

She looked around at the small crowd that had gathered. He saw her confusion.

"Do you remember what happened?" he asked.

"Karen?" she said and tried to sit up.

"I'm right here," the woman who'd been with Blythe answered. "I'm fine." She didn't sound fine though. She sounded scared. Her skirt was torn, her top soiled, and like Blythe she'd scraped her elbow and arm when Logan had thrown himself at them, knocking all three of them out of the way of the pickup.

Logan could still hear the roar of the engine, the sound of the tires on the pavement, and see the truck bearing down on the two women crossing the empty street.

"Okay, everybody stand back, please." Sheriff McCall Crawford worked her way through the small crowd as Logan was helping Blythe to her feet. "Someone tell me what happened here."

A shopkeeper told the sheriff what he'd seen. "It appeared the pickup purposely tried to run the two women down."

Blythe leaned into Logan, clearly still shaken. He put his arm around her and tried not to be angry with her, but it was hard not to be. She was determined to risk her life—and push him away. He wasn't having it after this. Whatever he had to do to keep her safe, he was doing it.

"Did anyone see the driver?" McCall asked.

Blythe looked to Karen who shook her head. "The sun was reflecting off the windshield."

"So you couldn't tell if it was a man or a woman?" the sheriff asked.

"No."

"What about you?" McCall asked Logan.

"I heard it coming but I was just trying to get to Blythe before the pickup hit her."

"None of you saw the pickup's license plate, either?" the sheriff asked.

More head shakes.

"It was covered with mud," Logan said. "The pickup was an older model Ford, brown, that's all I can tell you."

She nodded. "I'd suggest you see a doctor," she said to Blythe, who instantly started to argue.

"I agree," Logan spoke up. "She definitely needs her head examined. I'm taking her over to the emergency room now."

"Very funny, Logan," she said under her breath.

"Okay, if you remember anything..." McCall turned to Karen. "I'd like to speak with you if you don't mind."

"We'll be at the emergency room, if you need us," Logan said. "I'll see that Blythe is safe from now on whether she likes it or not."

He'd expected Blythe to argue and was surprised when she didn't. Had it finally sunk in that she was in serious danger?

Blythe glanced around. "Where is Karen?" she asked.

"She left with the sheriff," Logan said.

"I was hoping to at least say goodbye," Blythe said.

"Sorry, but I think she wants to put as much distance between the two of you as she can. Apparently she's having trouble with the idea of someone almost killing her—unlike you."

* * *

It wasn't until they reached the hospital that Blythe finally felt her scraped elbow and the ache in her hip where she'd hit the pavement. Logan had refused to leave her side, standing in the corner of the emergency room watching the doctor check her over.

The incident had scared him badly. She could see that he was still worried about her. There was a stubborn set to his jaw that told her he'd meant what he'd said about not leaving her side. The thought warmed her and frightened her. Whoever had tried to run her down today would be back. She was determined that Logan Chisholm not be in the line of fire when that happened.

"No concussion," the doctor said. "I'll have the nurse put something on the scrapes and you are good to go."

As the doctor left, Logan stepped over to her bed. She looked into his handsome face and saw both anger and relief. He'd hurled himself at her and Karen, throwing them out of the way, risking his own life to save hers. Could she love this man any more?

"You saved my life," she said.

He chuckled. "Doesn't that mean you owe me some debt for eternity?"

She knew what was coming. "I hate that you risked your life today because of me. I can't let you keep doing that." He could have been killed today. Karen, too.

"How do you plan to stop me?" he asked, leaning toward her.

She felt her breath catch, her heart a rising thunder in her chest as he leaned down, his lips hovering just a heartbeat away from her own before he kissed her. Her pulse leaped beneath her skin. But when she reached to cup the back of his neck and keep his mouth on hers, he pulled back.

"You are coming home with me or I'm moving into your apartment," he said. "Which is it going to be?"

She could see that there was no changing his mind. "I've missed the ranch and the horses. I've missed you, too." All true. "But Logan—"

"Then it's my place," Logan said, cutting her off.

AFTER THE SHERIFF'S VISIT ABOUT Aggie's murder, Hoyt had insisted on staying at Emma's side until the new housekeeper arrived. He took several weapons from his safe and dragged her out to the barn for more target practice.

"I want you to be able to shoot without hesitation," he told her, thrusting a pistol into her hand.

"I can shoot and you already gave me a gun," she said. "That's not what you want me to be able to do."

"No," he agreed meeting her gaze. "I want you to be able to kill if you have to and without a second thought."

Anyone could be taught to shoot a weapon. Killing, well, that was something else.

"What about you?" Emma asked after shooting several pistols and proving that she could hit anything she aimed at.

"I'm not worried about me," he said.

"I am." She looked into his handsome face, saw how much this had aged him. They'd been so happy when they'd first married—before Aggie Wells had come back into his life first with accusations of murder and then with her crazy story about Hoyt's first wife being alive and a killer.

"Can you kill her?" Emma asked him.

His gaze locked with hers. She saw that he wanted to argue that his first wife was already dead. But maybe even he wasn't so sure now.

"I would do anything to keep you from being hurt. *Anything.*" He pulled her into his arms and held her so tight she couldn't breathe.

He believed he could kill his first wife, his first love, a woman who had broken his heart in so many ways.

But Emma prayed he would never have to look into Laura's eyes and pull the trigger. If anyone had to do it, Emma hoped it wasn't him.

She took the pistol he handed her and aimed at the target on the hay bale and fired. Bull's-eye. But could she put a bullet through another woman's heart?

"So did you see her?"

Buford smiled as his fourteen-year-old granddaughter Amy met him at his front door. "I saw her."

Since the call from the Whitehorse sheriff about an attempt on JJ's life, he'd been distracted with the case. He'd forgotten that this granddaughter knew he'd been to Whitehorse to see her music idol.

"Is she more beautiful in person than even on television?"

"I couldn't say. She's quite attractive." He could tell his granddaughter had hoped for more. "She seems very nice."

Amy rolled her eyes. *"Nice?"*

He didn't know what else to say. "I *liked* her."

That too met with an eye roll. "You like everyone."

If only that were true.

"Can't you even tell me what she looked like? Pretend it's a description of one of your criminals," his granddaughter persisted.

He thought for a moment. "She's tall and slim and has really amazing eyes. The color of…"

"Worn blue jeans?"

He nodded smiling. "She was wearing jeans, a Western shirt, blue I think, and red cowboy boots. Her hair is dark and long and looks natural. And she just learned how to ride a horse."

Amy seemed pleased to hear that. "Did she say anything about when she would be singing again?"

"No. I think it could be a while." If ever. "She's taking a break. Waitressing at a café in Whitehorse."

"That is so cool," Amy exclaimed excitedly. "Can you imagine walking into a café in the middle of Montana and *JJ* was the one who took your order?"

He couldn't. "Are you still listening to Jett Atkins's music?" He was afraid if he told her how much he disliked Jett, it would only make her like the man's music simply out of rebellion.

"I don't like him as well as JJ."

Buford was glad to hear that.

"He really needs a new hit."

"What about that one you played for me?" He'd heard it several times on the alternative radio station since this whole thing started with JJ. He'd been listening to the station realizing it was high time he knew what his granddaughter listened to. "What was the name of that song again?"

"Poor Little Paper Doll." She said it as if she couldn't believe he had forgotten. "That song is really *old,*" she said. "It came out in 2002!" The way she said it, 2002 was centuries ago. He supposed it seemed that way to a fourteen-year-old.

"Hasn't he had other hits?" He realized how little he knew about the music business, just as he'd been told numerous times lately.

"Not really. Especially lately. His songs haven't been very good. I read online that his sales are lagging and his last concert didn't even sell out," she said.

Interesting, he thought. Jett hadn't had a hit for a while and his career was faltering. He said he didn't know why Martin Sanderson had invited him to Montana, but of course he could have been lying about that.

What if Martin was putting some kind of pressure on *him?*

But what could that have to do with JJ?

Buford shook his head. He was too tired to think about it anymore tonight.

"It's funny, the songs that did well for Jett were nothing like the ones he's been singing lately," Amy said thoughtfully as they went to find her grandmother and see what was for supper. "Maybe he's writing his own songs." Apparently seeing that her grandfather had lost interest, she added, "Maybe his songwriter died. Or was *murdered.*" She'd always known how to get Buford's attention.

* * *

"What's wrong?" Blythe asked, sitting up in bed to find Logan at the dark window looking out.

"One of the horses got out," he said. "I must not have closed the gate again. Nothing to worry about."

She watched him as he reached for his jeans, pulled them on, then leaned over the bed to give her a kiss.

"I'll be right back."

Blythe lay back down, content and snug under the soft, worn quilt. A cool breeze blew in one of the windows bringing the sweet new smells of the spring night. She smiled to herself, listening as she heard Logan go down the stairs and out the front door.

Rolling to her side, she placed a hand on his side of the bed. The sheets were still warm from where his naked body had been only minutes before. She breathed in his male scent and pulled his pillow under her head, unable to wipe the smile from her face.

This was a first for her, falling in love like this. She'd thought it would never happen. The men she'd met were more interested in JJ and being seen with her. She'd never met a man like Logan who loved Blythe, the girl she used to be.

A horse whinnied somewhere in the distance. She closed her eyes, wonderfully tired after their lovemaking, and let herself drift.

Logan would be back soon. She couldn't wait to feel his body next to her again, have him put his arms around her and hold her close as if he never wanted to let her go.

She just hoped he was right about them being safer

together. She couldn't bear it if something happened to
Logan because of her. Just as she couldn't bear being
out of his arms.

LOGAN WALKED ACROSS THE starlit yard. No moon tonight,
but zillions of stars glittered in a canopy of black velvet.
Dew sparkled in the grass, the starlight bathing the
pasture in silver.

He had pulled on his jeans and boots, but hadn't
bothered with a shirt. The air chilled his skin and he
couldn't wait to get back to Blythe. He smiled to himself as he thought of her, but then sobered as he remembered that she was a star.

Maybe she thought she didn't want to go back to it
now, but she would. She would miss being up on stage,
singing for thousands of screaming fans. Living out
here in the middle of Montana certainly paled next to
that. Right now, all of this was something new and different—just like him.

She was living her childhood dream of riding off
into the sunset on the back of a horse with a cowboy.
But that dream would end as the realization of a cowboy's life sunk in. He didn't kid himself that even the
fact that he'd fallen in love with her wouldn't change
that.

The thought startled him—just as the horse did as it
came out of the eerie pale darkness. It was the big bay,
and as it thundered past him, he saw that its eyes were
wide with fear.

The horse shied away. Something in the darkness

had startled the big bay. He'd never seen a rattlesnake near the corral at night, but he supposed it was possible.

Watching where he was walking, he moved closer to the open gate. The barn cast a long dark shadow over most of the corral and the horses inside it.

He heard restless movement. Something definitely had the horses spooked. As he neared the gate, he looked around for the shovel he'd left leaning against the post earlier. If there was a rattler in the corral tonight, the shovel would come in handy. But as he neared the corral, Logan saw with a frown that the shovel wasn't where he'd left it.

Something moved off to his left in the shadowed darkness of the barn and for a moment he thought it was another one of the horses loose.

The blow took him by surprise. He heard a clang rattle through his head, realization a split-second behind the shovel blade striking his skull.

The force of it knocked him forward. He stumbled, his legs crumbling under him as he fell face-first into the dirt.

BUFORD COULDN'T SLEEP. IT was this damned case. Slipping out of bed, careful not to wake his wife, he went to his computer. Something his granddaughter had said kept nagging at him.

First he checked to see when Jett's hit song, "Poor Little Paper Doll," came out. Six months after Tough as Nails broke up. Six months after Jett and JJ were "discovered" by Martin Sanderson.

Did that mean something?

He looked at the time line he'd made of the lives of the former members of the band. The only musician whose life changed at that time was Lisa "Luca" Thomas. She'd apparently come into money.

He checked his watch. It was late, but not that late, he told himself. He was afraid this couldn't wait. He called his friend who worked in the U.S. Treasury Department and explained that it was a matter of life and death and there wasn't time to go through "proper" channels.

"Lisa 'Luca' Thomas was employed as a songwriter. Ten years ago? She had a very good year with her songwriting."

"Who paid her the most?"

"Martin Sanderson."

He hung up and called the deputy he'd had working on the backgrounds of his suspects—the former members of the Tough as Nails band as well as Jett Akins. So far, the deputy hadn't come up with anything of real interest, but Buford had told him to keep digging until he did.

"I just put what I found on your desk at the office," the deputy said. "It's a birth certificate."

"Give it to me in a nutshell," Buford snapped.

"Betsy Harper Lee had a baby seven months after the band broke up," the deputy said.

"And I care about this why?"

"At the time the band broke up, according to Jett, who I called to confirm this, he and Betsy were hooking up. She hadn't even met her soon-to-be husband. Jett was the father of the baby Betsy was carrying. I suspected that might be the case when I saw the baby's middle name: Ray, Jett's real name."

"Did Jett know she was pregnant?" Buford asked.

"He did. He came up with all kinds of reasons he couldn't 'do the right thing' ten years ago, but the bottom line was that he left her high and dry because of his career—and he was with JJ by then."

Who would Betsy blame for the father of her baby leaving her? Not Jett—but the woman she believed had stolen him from her: JJ.

Now too wound-up to quit, Buford hung up and called the dispatcher to see if any of the rental agencies had gotten back to him.

"There is a message on your desk. Four different rental agencies called. All four of the names you gave them rented vehicles," the dispatcher said.

"Does it say what kind of cars they rented?" he asked. It did.

Only one had rented a pickup.

BLYTHE WOKE WITH A START. She hadn't intended to fall asleep, wanting to wait until Logan returned. The bed felt cold, the air coming in the window sending a chill over her bare flesh. She started to pull up the quilt to cover her shoulders and arms when she heard what had awakened her.

The phone was ringing downstairs.

She glanced at the clock on the nightstand next to the bed.

11:10 p.m.?

She blinked in confusion. Logan had gone to check

the horses a little after ten. He hadn't returned from putting the horse back in the corral?

The phone rang again.

Something was wrong. Hurriedly she sat up and swung her legs over the side of the bed to reach for Logan's robe. As she hurried out of the room and started down the stairs, the phone rang again.

"Logan?" She thought he might have come back in and decided to sleep on the couch for some reason. But he would have heard the phone, wouldn't he?

The whole house felt empty and cold. Starlight shone in through the windows, casting the living room in a pale otherworldly light as she came down the stairs.

As the phone rang again, it took her a moment to find it. She hadn't even realized that Logan had a landline. Another ring. She realized the sound was coming from the kitchen. From the moonlight spilling in the window, she saw the phone on the kitchen wall, an old-fashioned wall mount.

She snatched up the phone. "Hello?"

"JJ?" The voice was gruff and familiar and yet it took her a moment to place it. She hadn't been sure who might be calling this time of the night—and somehow she'd expected it would be Logan, though that made little sense. He'd only gone out to put the horses back in. Unless there was a phone out in the barn.

"I'm sorry to wake you. Is Logan there?" Sheriff Buford asked. There was an urgency to his tone that sent her heart pounding harder.

"No, I…he went out to check the horses and he

hasn't come back. I thought it might be him calling from the barn—"

"Listen to me," the sheriff snapped. "You have to get out of—"

Blythe heard the creak of the old kitchen floor behind her. As she turned, a hand snatched the phone from her and hung it up. She stumbled back as the kitchen light was snapped on, blinding her for an instant, as the last person she'd expected to see stepped from the shadows.

"What are you…" The rest of her words trailed off as she saw the gun.

Chapter Thirteen

"Thought I'd left? Or thought I'd forgiven you?" Karen asked as she leveled the gun at her.

Blythe remembered that bitter edge she'd heard in Karen's voice. She hadn't forgotten or forgiven. "But that truck. It almost hit us both."

Her old friend smiled. "Nice touch, huh. I thought you would appreciate the drama. I certainly lived through enough of yours when we were kids. Remember all the nights you used to crawl in my bedroom window to get away from one of your mother's drunk boyfriends?"

Until one night one of Blythe's mother's boyfriends followed her and threatened to go after Karen if she ever went to her house in the middle of the night again. That's when Blythe had started going to her own bed at night with a knife under the pillow.

"You had to know how much I appreciated that. I don't know what I would have done without you." She thought she heard a sound outside. Logan could be coming in that door at any moment.

"Until you got the chance to make something of yourself and left me behind," Karen snapped.

"I didn't want to. I told Martin I wouldn't go without you."

Karen seemed surprised by that. "What did he say?"

"He told me that he'd already offered you a music contract, but that you'd turned it down. Are you telling me he lied about that?"

"It's true I turned down his offer."

"Karen, why would you do that? Martin told me that you were his first choice because you were the one with all the talent."

Tears welled in her eyes. "Because of you. I couldn't leave you and the band."

Blythe studied her in the harsh glow of the overhead kitchen light. She could see the clock out of the corner of her eye. Logan should be coming back at any moment.

"He won't be coming," Karen said with a smile.

"What did you do to him?" Blythe cried, and took a step toward her.

Karen waved her back with the gun. "Don't worry. I didn't kill him. He's tied up out in the barn. I didn't want him interrupting our reunion. You did plan on the old band doing that reunion tour, didn't you, *JJ?*"

"That was Martin's doing. Not mine. He knew how much you all resented me. I'm sure the twisted bastard was hoping one of you would want to kill me."

"Or maybe he knew all along it would be me," Karen said. She hadn't let the gun in her hand waver for an instant. There was a determination in her eyes that Blythe remembered from when they were kids.

"I'm going to be someone someday," Karen used to

say. "Those people who look down their noses at me now will regret it one day. I want fame and fortune. I want people to recognize me when I walk down the street and say, 'Isn't that her? You know that famous singer.'"

Blythe's dream had been to get out of the desert trailer park and away from her drunk mother's boyfriends. She hadn't dreamed of fame and fortune and yet she'd gotten both.

"You could have had fame and fortune just like you used to say you wanted when we were kids. You turned it down, and not because of me."

Karen started to argue, but Blythe cut her off.

"Martin always said that what I lacked in talent I made up for in guts. He said it was too bad you were just the opposite."

"Don't I look like I have guts?" Karen demanded and took a threatening step toward her. Karen aimed the gun at Blythe's heart. "If you think I won't kill you, you're wrong. I can't bear the thought of you living the life that should have been mine any longer."

"I'm a waitress now, Karen," Blythe snapped. "You want that life, go for it."

The gun blast was deafening in the small kitchen.

LOGAN WOKE TO THE FEEL OF THE cold hard ground beneath him and a killer headache. For a moment, he couldn't remember what had happened. If not for the ropes binding him, he might have thought one of the horses had clipped him and he'd hit his head when he went down.

He tried to sit up, straining against the ropes around his wrists and ankles. His head swam at the effort, but as his thoughts cleared, he let out a curse. Blythe.

Whoever had hit him and tied him up was after Blythe.

Rolling to his side, he looked around for something to free himself. In the corner, he spotted an old scythe that he sometimes used to cut weeds behind the barn. He began to work his way over to it, scooting on the cold earth, his mind racing.

He remembered that he'd come out to put the horses back in the pasture. He'd thought he'd left the gate open. It wouldn't have been the first time one of the horses had gotten out. Even when he realized that something was spooking the horses, he thought it must be a rattler.

Never had he thought anyone would come after Blythe out here. His mistake. One he prayed wouldn't cost her her life.

He reached the scythe, knocked it over and positioned it between his wrists as he began to saw. He couldn't believe anyone would want to harm Blythe, certainly not one of her former band members, and yet someone had taken a shovel to the back of his head and left him hog-tied in the barn.

What were they going to do to Blythe?

Not kill her. No, just scare her. Logan desperately wanted to believe that in the end, they wouldn't be able to hurt her. But then he had no concept of the kind of hatred that could bring another person to kill.

Logan sawed through the ropes on his wrist and was

reaching for the scythe to cut the bindings around his ankles when he heard the gunshot. His heart dropped.

KAREN SMILED AS A CERAMIC container on the kitchen counter exploded, sending shards flying and startling Blythe. "I planned all of this. Hired someone to make it look like someone else from the band had tried to run us down on the street. I know Martin thought I was a coward, that I blamed you because I didn't go for what I wanted ten years ago and instead let you take it from me. Martin told me to my face just before I killed him."

Blythe stared at Karen in shock. "I thought his death was ruled a suicide."

"He said he was going to kill himself when I found him that morning about to write his suicide note," Karen said with a smile. "But we both knew he wouldn't have called me to meet him over at the house unless he lacked the courage to do it. He had the gun pointed at his chest, but I was the one who had to press the trigger. He goaded me into it because he didn't have the guts to do it himself. I was the last person he saw."

"Oh, Karen." She felt sick as she stumbled back against the kitchen table. Her fingers felt the smooth brim of Logan's Stetson and her heart lurched at the thought of him. She prayed Karen was telling the truth and hadn't hurt him.

"You're the one who left the note for me," she said, seeing it all now. "Martin must have told you I was there in another part of the house. All these years. You could have had a career. It didn't have to be either me or you."

"Do you know what makes me the angriest?" Karen said as if Blythe hadn't spoken. "You had it all and you were going to throw it away. Martin told me how you didn't appreciate it. You had everything I'd dreamed of and yet it meant nothing to you."

"Karen, that's not—"

"Don't bother to lie. You took what was mine." Her face twisted in a mask of fury. "Martin was right. You don't deserve to live."

Blythe had only a split second to react as Karen brought the gun up and squeezed the trigger. The Stetson brim was already in the fingers of her right hand. She drew it from behind her and hurled the hat at Karen as she dived for the floor.

LOGAN HURRIEDLY CUT THROUGH the ropes. As he stumbled to his feet, he felt the effects of the blow to his head. He could barely breathe, his fear was so great, but it was the dizziness that made him grab hold of the barn wall for a moment. His vision clearing, he raced toward his pickup and the shotgun that hung in the rack in the back window.

Two gunshots. His heart was in his throat as he saw that the kitchen light was on. But he saw no one as he quietly opened his pickup door and took down his shotgun. From behind the seat, he found the box of shells and popped one in each side of the double barrels. Snapping it shut, he headed for the front door.

He knew he couldn't go in blasting. If Blythe wasn't already dead—

The thought clutched at his heart. He'd brought

her out here so he could protect her. If he'd gotten her killed—

He eased open the front door and instantly heard what sounded like a scuffle just inside.

BLYTHE WASN'T SURE IF SHE'D been hit or not. She felt the hard floor as she hit her already scraped elbow. But even that pain didn't register at first as she knocked Karen's feet out from under her.

Karen came down hard next to her. A loud "oof!" came out of her as she hit the floor. Blythe saw that there was a red welt on Karen's cheek where the Stetson brim must have hit her.

Blythe grabbed for the gun, but Karen reacted faster than she'd expected. She kicked out at Blythe, driving her back as she brought up the gun and aimed it at her head.

As Karen scrambled to her feet, Blythe slowly got to hers.

"I'm sorry this is how it has to end," Blythe said as she saw the front door slowly swing open behind Karen. "I never wanted to hurt you. You were like a sister to me. I missed you so much. I can't tell you how many times I wanted to pick up the phone and call you."

"Why didn't you?" Karen demanded, sounding close to tears. Her arm was bleeding from where she'd gotten skinned-up earlier on the main drag in Whitehorse. She must have hit it when she fell, Blythe thought as she tried to think about anything but Logan.

He had slipped in through the front door, a shotgun

in his hands, and was now moving up behind Karen. He motioned for her to keep talking.

"I didn't think you would want to hear from me after the band broke up," she said. "I blamed myself for leaving it and leaving you. I guess I also didn't believe Martin that you'd turned down an offer to do what I was doing. I thought he'd lied. It wouldn't have been the first time."

Logan was now right behind Karen, practically breathing down her neck. She was crying, big fat tears running down her face.

"He was right, you know?" Karen said and made a swipe at her tears with her free hand. "I was afraid that I wouldn't be good enough to make it. I hoped you would fail but when you didn't..." She seemed to get hold of herself, inhaling and letting out a long sigh. "It's too late now. I've burned too many bridges. This has to end here. You and me. Just as it always should have been."

Something in Karen's gaze suddenly changed. Blythe saw Logan raise the shotgun and cried out to warn him as Karen suddenly spun around.

Blythe felt her legs give under her. She dropped to her knees as she watched Logan bring the butt of the shotgun down on the side of Karen's head. As she crumbled like a ragdoll, she managed to get off another shot. It whizzed past Logan, missing him only by inches, before shattering something in the living room.

In the distance, she heard the sound of sirens and remembered the call from Sheriff Buford Olson earlier. He must have called the local sheriff, McCall Crawford, for moments later the ranch yard filled with flashing lights and the sound of doors slamming and running feet on the porch steps.

Blythe buried her face in Logan's shoulder as he dropped to his knees beside her. His breath was ragged, his heart a drum in his chest as he dragged her to him. She heard his voice break with emotion as he thanked God that she was alive.

Then he lifted her face to his and told her he loved her.

Epilogue

"If I could have your attention please." Logan rose from his chair at the long table in the dining room of the main house at Chisholm ranch. He touched his knife to his wineglass again. A hush fell over the room as all eyes turned in his direction.

Blythe felt her heart kick up a beat as Logan smiled down at her. She wanted to pinch herself. So much had happened since that night in the kitchen. Everything about JJ and the past had come out. Logan's family had been so supportive, just the memory brought tears to her eyes.

They'd spent the rest of that night giving their statements to the sheriff, having the doctor check Logan over to make sure he didn't have a concussion and filling his family in on JJ and everything else that had happened.

Sheriff Buford Olson had picked up Loretta and charged her with attempted murder after discovering that she'd rented the pickup and had been the driver in the near hit-and-run. Karen had paid Loretta to do it, but Loretta told Buford that she'd been happy to. In fact, she'd done her best to hit both of them.

Karen had hired herself a good lawyer. When Blythe had tried to visit her in jail, Karen had refused to see her. As she'd left the sheriff's department, she didn't look back. She was through blaming herself for the events of the past.

Before he died, Martin Sanderson had also released Jett from his contract, but Jett was quickly finding out that no other recording studio was interested. On top of that, Betsy had produced a sworn affidavit from their deceased band member Lisa "Luca" Thomas, stating that Jett had stolen songs from her and what she'd been paid for them—after he'd recorded the songs as his own. Her estate was suing Jett for full disclosure.

That had pretty much driven a stake through the last of his singing career.

Blythe had been glad to see that Betsy had more backbone than any of them had seen before. She'd known that Betsy was pregnant all those years ago before the band broke up. But if her oldest son was Jett's, then it was a secret Betsy intended to take to her grave.

A few days ago, Blythe had been sitting on the porch in the shade after a long horseback ride with Logan when he joined her.

"I love you," he said. Blythe started to speak, but he stopped her.

"You don't have to say anything. I know that staying here, on this ranch, in the middle of nowhere is the last thing in the world you want to do."

"Logan—"

He touched a finger to her lips. "Let me finish. I

didn't tell you I love you to try to get you to stay. I just wanted you to know that if you ever need to get away from your life again, I'll be here."

She smiled and shook her head. "I'm not going to want to escape my life again. All of this has helped me know what I want to do with the rest of it." She touched his handsome face, cupping his strong jaw with her palm. "I love you, Logan Chisholm, and there is no place I want to be other than right here with you."

He'd stared at her in surprise. "What about your career—"

"Martin freed me from my contract, so I do still have my singing career if I wanted it. But since climbing on the back of your motorcycle that day over in the Flathead, I've known that the only singing I want to do is to my babies. You do want children, don't you?"

"THERE'S SOMETHING I NEED to ask this woman," Logan said now as he reached down and took Blythe's hand. "Jennifer Blythe James, would you be my wife?"

Blythe felt tears blur her eyes as she looked around the table and saw all the smiling welcoming faces. Then she turned her face up to Logan. "There is nothing I would love more," she said.

He dragged her to her feet and into his arms. She leaned into him, felt his strength and that of his family around them, all the things a good marriage needed.

The room burst with applause and cheers around them as Logan kissed her. Blythe could see their children running through this big house, all the holidays and birthdays, all the cousins, aunts and uncles.

She'd dreamed of a big family, but the Chisholms were bigger and more loving than any she had ever dreamed possible.

When Logan finally released her, she found herself hugged by everyone in the room. Emma was last. She'd cupped Blythe's shoulders in her hands and just looked at her for a long moment.

"You are going to make the most beautiful bride and such a good wife to our Logan," she said, her voice breaking with emotion. "Welcome to the family." Emma pulled her into a hug.

Through her tears, Blythe saw her future husband standing nearby looking at her as if he would always see her as she was now. She smiled back, picturing getting old with this man. Yes, after all the fame and fortune, this was exactly where she wanted to be.

HER NAME WAS NOW CYNTHIA CROWLEY. She'd picked the name out of thin air—just as she did most of her names.

She thought of it as reinventing herself. She cut her hair, dyed it, got different colored contact lenses, changed her makeup, her address, became the woman she imagined Cynthia Crowley was. A widow with no family and no real means of support.

Laura had first discovered in high school drama class that she could don a disguise like an outer shell. She'd loved acting and she was good at it. Everyone said she seemed to transform into her character. The truth was, her characters had felt more real to her than whoever she'd been before she pulled on their skin.

She liked to think of herself as a chameleon. Or a snake that was forever shedding its skin. She had changed character so many times that some days she could hardly remember that young woman who'd married Hoyt Chisholm. Laura suspected though that Mrs. Laura Chisholm had been as big a fake as Cynthia Crowley was now.

Women did that when they married for life. They became who their husbands *thought* they had married. That's what she had done with Hoyt. She'd played the role of his wife. At least for a while.

It was no wonder that her life had led her to the special effects department of several movie studios in California. It was amazing how the new products could transform an actor. She especially loved a type of substance that reminded her of the glue she'd used in grade school. As a special effects makeup artist, she had worked with actors to make them look old and wrinkled or badly scarred.

The work was rewarding. She loved what she did and often experimented with her own disguises. But ultimately, there was only one constant in her life. Hoyt Chisholm.

Laura remembered the first time she'd seen Hoyt. She'd known then that she would love him until the day she died. She'd also known that he would never love her as much as she loved him. It had broken her heart every moment she'd been with him. That was why she hadn't been able to stay. It had been too painful knowing that one day he would see the real her and hate her.

She was tortured by the way other women had

looked at him. It had been impossible not to imagine him with one of them instead of her. Hoyt would become angry when she'd voice her fears and she'd feel another piece of her heart gouged away by his lack of understanding.

Once he'd decided to adopt the boys, she'd lost more of him. He'd actually thought the boys would bring the two of them closer, but when she'd seen his love for babies that weren't even his own blood, she'd felt herself losing more and more of him. He tried to make it up to her, trying so hard it made her hurt even worse. She'd seen him start to pull away from her and knew she had to escape before it got any worse.

Divorce was out of the question. She would always be his only wife till death parted them. She could have warned him not to ever remarry before she faked her death that day on Fort Peck Reservoir. But Hoyt wouldn't have understood. You had to love someone so much it hurt to understand.

She'd known he would remarry. She'd thought he would have to wait seven years to have her declared dead. But he'd found a way around it, marrying that bitch Tasha. Unlike her, Tasha had shared Hoyt's love of horses. Oh, the horrible pain of watching the two of them together, until one day she couldn't take it any longer and had rigged Tasha's saddle.

After that, she'd hoped Hoyt wouldn't marry again. But Hoyt hadn't been able to resist the young woman who'd been helping take care of his boys. Krystal appealed to Hoyt's need to protect a woman in trouble.

He would have continued to try to save Krystal if Laura hadn't helped him by getting rid of her for good.

From a safe distance, she had watched him raise the boys alone, all six of them, and build an empire. She'd been proud of him, had actually loved him more.

Then Emma had come along.

Laura shook her head. Just the thought made her hands ball into fists, her jaw tightening, her heart on fire.

Hoyt was in love. Or so he thought. She knew the power of love, but it was a weak emotion compared to hate. Hate, now there was something with substance, something you could feel deep in your bone marrow, something to live for.

Laura lived now for only one thing. To see Emma Chisholm dead and gone. But this time she thought Hoyt might have to go, as well. Maybe his sons and their fiancées too. Maybe it was time to finally end this pain once and for all. If only Hoyt had loved her and only her.

As she parked her car and got out, it looked as if they were having a party, but she knew Emma made a big deal out of suppers at the ranch. Everyone was here. Perfect.

She stood for a moment, looking at the huge house all ablaze with lights, remembering when it had been hers and Hoyt's.

Then she made her way up to the front door and rang the doorbell. It would be her house again in a few moments, she thought with a crooked smile.

* * *

When the doorbell rang, everyone turned in surprise toward the front door.

"Are you expecting someone?" Emma asked her husband.

Hoyt shook his head. "Unless it's the live-in housekeeper. She wasn't supposed to be here until tomorrow though. I'll go see."

Emma asked her future daughters-in-law to serve dessert and went into the living room. Hoyt was already at the door, opening it as the bell rang again.

Standing back, Emma waited. She wondered what this woman Hoyt had hired to babysit her would be like. Dreaded, was more like it. Older, he'd said. Experienced, he'd said.

Emma feared she would be dull as dirt, when what she needed was to kick up her heels after everything she'd been through since marrying Hoyt.

But she wasn't going to complain. If the woman wasn't any fun, then Emma would find a way to sneak away from her.

Bracing herself, Emma watched Hoyt open the door. He hadn't turned on the porch light so she couldn't see the woman standing on their doorstep clearly.

"Come on in, Cynthia," Hoyt said. "We expected you tomorrow, but tonight is fine. You're just in time for dessert."

"Call me Mrs. Crowley," the woman said in a low hoarse voice. She spoke strangely as if out of one side of her mouth. Had the woman had a stroke?

And as she stepped into the light, Emma saw that

her face was badly scarred on one side as if she'd been burned in a fire.

"Whatever you prefer," Hoyt said and turned to see Emma standing at some distance behind him. "Mrs. Crowley, I'd like you to meet my wife, Emma."

The woman looked up then and Emma felt a chill race through her. One of the woman's eyes was a dark brown. The other one on the side that had been burned was completely white and sightless.

"I know I don't look like much," the woman said in her hoarse voice. "But I'm a hard worker."

"I'm sure you are," Emma said stepping to her to take her hand. "Welcome to Chisholm ranch."

The woman's grip was strong. "Thank you, Mrs. Chisholm."

She hated that the woman was hard to look at because of her injury, but she knew over time, they would all adapt to it, just as Cynthia Crowley had herself.

"Please call me Emma," she said warmly.

"Don't you worry, Emma. I am much stronger than I look. Before long, I promise you'll be surprised at what I'm capable of doing."

* * * * *

SUSPENSE

Harlequin®

INTRIGUE®

COMING NEXT MONTH
AVAILABLE APRIL 10, 2012

#1341 SON OF A GUN
Big "D" Dads
Joanna Wayne

#1342 SECRET HIDEOUT
Cooper Security
Paula Graves

#1343 MIDWIFE COVER
Cassie Miles

#1344 BABY BREAKOUT
Outlaws
Lisa Childs

#1345 PUREBRED
The McKenna Legacy
Patricia Rosemoor

#1346 RAVEN'S COVE
Jenna Ryan

Harlequin®

ROMANTIC
SUSPENSE

Danger is hot on their heels!

Catch the thrill with author

LINDA CONRAD

Chance, Texas

Sam Chance, a U.S. marshal in the Witness Security
Service, is sworn to protect Grace Brown and her
one-year-old son after Grace testifies against an infamous
drug lord and he swears revenge. With Grace on the edge of
fleeing, Sam knows there is only one safe place he can take
her—home. But when the danger draws near, it's not just
Sam's life on the line but his heart, too.

Watch out for

Texas Baby Sanctuary

Available April 2012

Texas Manhunt

Available May 2012

Taft Bowman knew he'd ruined any chance he'd had for happiness with Laura Pendleton when he drove her away years ago...and into the arms of another man, thousands of miles away. Now she was back, a widow with two small children...and despite himself, he was starting to believe in second chances.

Harlequin Special® Edition® presents a new installment in USA TODAY *bestselling author RaeAnne Thayne's miniseries,* THE COWBOYS OF COLD CREEK.

Enjoy a sneak peek of A COLD CREEK REUNION

Available April 2012 from Harlequin® Special Edition®

A younger woman stood there, and from this distance he had only a strange impression, as though she was somehow standing on an island of calm amid the chaos of the scene, the flashing lights of the emergency vehicles, shouts between his crew members, the excited buzz of the crowd.

And then the woman turned and he just about tripped over a snaking fire hose somebody shouldn't have left there.

Laura.

He froze, and for the first time in fifteen years as a firefighter, he forgot about the incident, his mission, just what the hell he was doing here.

Laura.

Ten years. He hadn't seen her in all that time, since the week before their wedding when she had given him back his ring and left town. Not just town. She had left the whole damn country, as if she couldn't run far enough to get away from him.

Some part of him desperately wanted to think he had made some kind of mistake. It couldn't be her. That was just some other slender woman with a long sweep of honey-blond hair and big, blue, unforgettable eyes. But no. It was definitely Laura. Sweet and lovely.

Not his.

He was going to have to go over there and talk to her. He didn't want to. He wanted to stand there and pretend he hadn't seen her. But he was the fire chief. He couldn't hide out just because he had a painful history with the daughter of the property owner.

Sometimes he hated his job.

Will Taft and Laura be able to make the years recede...or is the gulf between them too broad to ever cross?

Find out in
A COLD CREEK REUNION
Available April 2012 from Harlequin® Special Edition®
wherever books are sold.

Celebrate the 30th anniversary
of Harlequin® Special Edition® with a bonus story
included in each Special Edition® book in April!